A S

MW01258052

Also by Andy Remic

A SONG FOR NO MAN'S LAND

ANDY REMIC

A TOM DOHERTY ASSOCIATES BOOK

NEW YORK

This is a work of fiction. All of the characters, organizations, and events portrayed in this novella are either products of the author's imagination or are used fictitiously.

A SONG FOR NO MAN'S LAND

Copyright © 2016 by Andy Remic

Cover art by Jeffrey Alan Love
Cover designed by Christine Foltzer

Edited by Lee Harris

All rights reserved.

A Tor.com Book
Published by Tom Doherty Associates, LLC
175 Fifth Avenue
New York, NY 10010

www.tor.com

Tor® is a registered trademark of Tom Doherty Associates, LLC.

ISBN 978-0-7653-8401-0 (ebook)
ISBN 978-0-7653-8787-5 (trade paperback)

First Edition: February 2016

D 0 9 8 7 6 5 4 3 2 1

This novella is dedicated to the soldiers who fought in the First World War

Author's Note

I have replaced the word "fuck" with "——" throughout the text, in the style of early World War I writings where soldiers self-censored; this has been done to help authenticate the text.

PART ONE

THE SOMME

THE FIGHTING COCKS PUBLIC HOUSE
KING'S CROSS, LONDON.
3RD. JANUARY, 1914.

HE LAY ON HIS back, mind reeling as bloodshot eyes focussed on stars flitting across the high, smoke-stained beams. Remnants of whisky tasted sour, a dead rat on his tongue, and he could hear the muffled public house sounds as if swimming under water, diving deep into a realm of bitter dreams.

The punch knocked Jones clean off his stool, splitting his lip and bruising his jaw; but as he lay, all eyes upon him, and a cold silence descended through the smoke like falling ash, he grinned—because he no longer cared. He had reached the nadir. He'd lost so much money, and they would be coming for him real soon, with balled fists and blazing eyes and harsh words, with bricks and helves, and the pain would follow... He'd follow sour whisky down a long tunnel into oblivion darkness. Just like the old days. Back in Wales. In the woods. Hunted by the Skogsgrå.

Damn and bloody hell!

But now, ha yes, now! He would enjoy the drink

whilst he could, savour the hot sweet liquor ... and if his strength didn't fail him—as so often it did—find a willing woman for the night.

"Come on; up, lad." A large, bearded man helped Jones to his feet, and the young gambler stood, swaying and rubbing his injured jaw. He hiccupped, then staggered to the bar.

"Another whisky, bartender!"

"Get that ——er out of 'ere!" growled the stocky Cockney landlord.

A tall American with angry eyes and clenched fists moved towards Jones, but the bearded man held up a fist, and in silence, the American subsided, finished his beer, and left the pub. Two minutes later, the gambler was out in the rain, supported by the bearded man, whose face was a scowl.

"Where you staying, lad?"

The reply was a mumble of unrecognisable words. Then Jones's face suddenly brightened and he managed, "I need a drink. More whisky! Hey ... where are we going?" He paused, feet kicking the cobbles as he was half-helped, half-dragged along. "Where am I? Who are *you*?"

The man smiled. "I'm Charlie Bainbridge. Charlie to my friends. Nice to meet you. You were about to get a royal kicking in there, son, and I can't stand seeing a drunk man battered for no reason. Especially by an *Amer-*

ican."

"It . . . would have been all right, Charlie." Jones waved a hand, as if swatting away a wasp.

"That's as may be. But you sure can't be having any more whisky down your throat, or you'll be decorating the pavement with your supper! Anyway, come on, lad, what's your name?"

The gambler thought for a while. "I'm Robert Jones. And I ain't had my supper," he mumbled, coughing and wiping his nose on his sleeve.

Bainbridge nodded, and continued to drag Jones along the cobbles, and finally dumped him on a scrubbed stone doorstep at the end of a terraced street. Jones reclined, eyes shut, mouth open, the stink of whisky strong on his breath.

"You've had a skinful, all right, lad," said Bainbridge, tugging a cigarette from his pocket, cupping it to his mouth, and lighting it with a flare that illuminated his dark, brooding eyes in thick eye sockets. "Maybe you should curl up and go to sleep right there? Damned if I can carry you all the way home."

Suddenly, there came a clattering of boots at the end of the street. A harsh voice bellowed, "You there!" and echoes bounced from house to house as long shadows stretched ahead.

Bainbridge blew smoke from his nose and picked a

bit of tobacco from the tip of his tongue with thick fingers. He watched as three large-set men pounded down the street, hobnailed boots heavy and scuffed, clothes rough and unwashed.

"You all right, gents?" asked Bainbridge, turning and placing himself between the half-conscious, grinning, oblivious figure of Jones, and the three men who slowed their run and stopped under the glow of a streetlamp.

"He owes Tyson a lot of money," said one man, who had a thick bull neck and shaved head. His eyes were small, like a pig's, and looked past Bainbridge to the slumbering gambler. "We've come to claim what is owed."

"Oh, yes?" said Bainbridge, drawing deeply on his cigarette. "Well, lads, I think he's in no position to pay just this minute. You can see that. Now, you come back in the morning, and he'll sort you out, I'm sure."

"You'd be Charlie Bainbridge, eh?" said the cocky newcomer with the bull neck, turning his head and fixing his piglet gaze on Bainbridge proper.

Bainbridge nodded, watching the leader of the three roll up his sleeves and crack his knuckles with a smile. "I have heard a lot about Charlie Bainbridge . . . I've heard you're quite a man with your fists?"

Bainbridge sighed, flicked away his cigarette, rolled back on his right hip and delivered a powerful hook to the jaw that sent a tooth skittering across the cobbles like a rolled die, and saw bull-neck twitching on the ground, piss staining his unwashed trousers. The other two men rushed in and shadows danced against the wall as Jones, who had been watching the glowing tip of Bainbridge's discarded cigarette, closed his eyes and began to snore.

THE FRENCH OFFENSIVE:
BATTLE OF FLERS-COURCELETTE.
16TH. SEPTEMBER 1916.

DISTANT MACHINE GUNS roared, like some great alien creature in agony. Rain lashed from unhealthy iron skies, caressed the upturned faces of soldiers praying to a god they no longer believed in for a miracle that couldn't happen.

A sudden explosion of mortar shell and the Tommies flinched—some half-ducking, fear etched clear on frightened young faces. Debris rained down behind the trench and the men let out deep sighs, turned pale faces to the sky once more, and gripped the slippery stocks of rifles in a desperate prayer of reassurance.

Explosions echoed, distant, muffled. The ground trembled like a virgin. Occasionally, there was a scream from *out there,* and whistles pierced the Stygian gloom from other parts of the trench as battalions headed out into the rain and the treacherous mud.

Tommies exchanged half-hearted jokes and anecdotes, laughed over-loud, and slapped one another on the back as guns roared and crumps shattered any illusion of safety.

Deep in the trench, two men stood slightly apart, talking quietly, refusing to be drawn into any false charade of happiness; one was a large man, his close-cropped hair stuck at irregular angles, his face ruddy with the glow of adrenalin and rising excitement, his knuckles white as they gripped the stock of his rifle. The other man was smaller in stature, his face pale, hair lank with falling rain and sticking to his forehead. They were waiting, waiting patiently. Out there, it seemed the whole world was waiting.

"I ——ing hate this," muttered Bainbridge after a period of silence, baring his teeth. "It's all arsapeek. I want to be over the top. I want to do it now!"

"It'll come soon enough," soothed Jones, brushing hair back from his forehead and rubbing his eyes with an oil-blackened hand. "When the brass hats sort their shit out."

"It's the waiting that's the worst. An eternity of waiting!"

Jones hoisted his SMLE, and at last the captain appeared, a drifting olive ghost from the false dusk. The whistle was loud, shrill, an unmistakable brittle signal, and the sergeant was there offering words of encouragement, his familiar voice steady, his bravery and solidity a rain-slick rock to which the limpets could cling.

The Tommies pulled on battered helmets, then Bainbridge led Jones towards the muddy ladders, and the men of the battalion climbed—some in silence, some still joking, most feeling the apprehension and a rising glow of almost painful wonder in their chests, in their hearts. Most of the men were new conscripts, a few were veterans; all felt the invasive and terrible fear of the moment.

Hands and boots slipped on muddy, wet rungs.

Overhead, shells screamed, cutting the sky in half as if it were the end of the world.

And then they were over the bags.

DIARY OF ROBERT JONES.
3RD. BATTALION ROYAL WELSH FUSILIERS.
16TH. SEPTEMBER 1916.

I'm off the whisky now, and this is making me push on, making me strive for a new beginning. I can't help feeling this is a mistake, though; I am out of place in a smart uniform, taking orders from the brass. And my haircut is ridiculous. No women for Rob Jones now!

I've learnt much from Bainbridge in this hole. He's taught me with his fist to lay off the whisky, as that's the reason I'm here. Him—he enjoys the fighting, I think. Another challenge for the warrior inside him. He's a born soldier.

I went into battle today, over the bags with the rest of the company and tasting fear and wishing like hell for just a sip of that warm heaven. It is strange, the things a man remembers when under pressure, pinned under gunfire, when suffering fear and disgust at a situation into which he is forced. I remember my wet boots, the bastards, soaked with mud and water because the trench had flooded. God, that stunk.

I remember the chats, lice in my hair, wriggling, and

cursing myself for not getting to the delouse.

I remember the rough texture of the wooden rungs on the ladder as I climbed to go over the bags, each rung a cheese grater, shredding my skin, dragging at my boots as if warning me not to go over the top.

It all seemed like a dream. Surreal.

The ground was churned mud, harsh, difficult to cross; the noise was like nothing I'd ever experienced before! The crack of rifles, the ping and whistle of bullets, the roar of machine guns from the Hun trench. My friends went down screaming in the mud, hands clawing at the ground; some were punched back screaming to the trench, their faces and chests torn open, showing ragged strips of meat, smashed-in skulls. Some vomited blood to the earth right there before me. And there was nothing I could do to help them, the poor bastards.

I pounded on beside Bainbridge, muscles hurting, mouth dry, and Bainbridge was shouting, shouting, always bloody shouting like a maniac! We ran past trees, stark, arthritic ghosts in the gloom, shot to hell and stinking a sulphur stink, a sad contrast to the bright woodlands of my youth in glorious Wales . . .

There were tanks—great, lumbering terrifying machines belching fumes and grinding through mud; we loved the tanks, though, because we used them for cover, ducked our heads behind their metal husks, breathed their stinking fumes, their unholy pollution as bullets rattled from iron hulls. I remember thinking how frightening they were, but not as frightening as the smash of crumps tearing holes in the ground; not as frightening as the continuous roar of those ——ing machine guns. The guns never seemed to stop, and I remember thinking each tiny click of that perpetual noise was a bullet leaving the chamber, a bullet that could smash away life, delivering death in a short, sharp, painful punch.

We—a few men from my battalion—reached an old barn or some similar kind of building; it surprised us, rearing suddenly out of the smoke-filled gloom, and we waited there to catch our breaths. I noticed nobody was telling jokes now. Nobody was ——ing smiling. I took the time to look in the men's faces, tried to imprint the images in my skull in case they were killed. I would have liked to remember them, remember them all—but out there, it was a sad dream.

I was despondent, feeling the whole world had forgotten us in that insane place of guns and mud and noise. The girls back home could never understand. How could they? All they saw were pictures of smart Tommies in their uniforms marching off to battle. The proud British Tommy! It made me want to puke.

We were forgotten, left there to fight an insane battle and die for something we did not understand, that no longer mattered. It was a terrifying thought and my head was spinning.

Most of all, I remember the fear. Like black oil smothering me.

And so I tried to escape, into dreams of childhood.

Back, to Dolwyddelan, and the wonderful woods near Gwydyr Forest where I played as a child, under the watchful, stern gaze of Yr Wyddfa, my sentinel.

Even back then, I never managed to grasp the truth, or the reality . . . But then, that was a million years ago.

At Flers-Courcelette, I would have sang to the Devil for a drink, and Bainbridge was good to me. He supported me, gave me help, urged me on when I thought I could go no further. Bainbridge was a true friend, and I thank him here in my diary—I thank him for keeping me off the whisky, and for keeping me alive.

Thank you, Charlie.

FLERS-COURCELETTE.
THE FIELD, 28TH. SEPTEMBER, 1916.

"COME ON, LAD," growled Bainbridge, placing his hand on Jones's shoulder. "Our brothers are fighting out there, getting outed, and we're crouched here like we're having a shit in a possie."

Jones nodded, took a long, deep breath, and looked around; most of the battalion had moved out again, and some of the tanks had foundered, sitting in the mud like stranded monsters, lurking in the mist, waiting for unsuspecting soldiers to creep past. Some revved engines, grinding, others were silent, squatting at fallen angles in shell holes, like broken siege engines.

Jones took hold of his rifle, spat, "Let's move, then," and followed Bainbridge out into the world of mud and smashed trees. They crept past a low wall of chewed stone, over corpses of fallen men like twisted dolls, and Jones kicked a length of barbed wire out of his path.

They were close to the enemy line now, could see the blackened smear across the earth like some great dark wound. Machine guns roared in bursts, and rifles cracked. The objective was simple—take the enemy communications trench. A simple order filled with clarity. Easy for the bastards to type on a clean white page back at HQ. But in the real world, out here, not quite such an easy task . . .

Bainbridge felt good. The fear and frustration of waiting had gone. The rush of the advance was with him, in his heart, in his mind—his rifle an extension of his person, a finely tuned tool of death at his fingertips. Somebody would pay for all that waiting, all that fear, all the lice. Somebody would pay for all the corpses. The bodies of dead friends, lost comrades. Somebody would pay in blood.

Jones felt a cold, creeping terror. His guts were churning. Every time he stepped over a corpse, the face like an anguished ghost, silently screaming, he felt himself die just a little bit more inside. There was no respect out here. No dignity.

"Bainbridge, slow down," he hissed, slipping in mud. He glanced left, could see other Tommies moving through the gloom of mist and gun smoke. There was a burst of machine gun fire, and he saw three men go down, arms flailing like rag dolls.

Bainbridge hit the ground on his belly. "Bastards." He gestured, and Jones slid up beside him.

They were close now. Could see the sandbags and barbed wire of the Hun trench.

"You ready, lad?"

Jones gave a silent nod.

They leapt over a low stone wall and charged. Rifle shots cracked ahead. Jones could see muzzle flash. Bainbridge got there first, fired a bullet through a German skull; other Tommies were behind them, screaming, charging. There was a gap in the wire caused by Allied crumps, and Bainbridge was through, leaping into the trench, boots stomping on duckboards. Jones jumped in after him, past sandbags, into ankle-deep water. Men were around him. The Hun! There was a pistol crack by his face, and he ducked, his own weapon striking out, butt smashing a German's cheekbone. The man went down, face broken, and this battle was suddenly an insane struggle with rifle butts and bayonets. A Hun loomed and Jones lunged with his bayonet, but the German grabbed Jones's coat, fingers surprisingly strong and refusing to let go. Jones stumbled backwards but the Hun released, and Jones hammered his rifle butt into the man's face again and again and again, the soldier was screaming, but Jones couldn't hear it; the soldier had a knife in his hand, flashing up from nowhere. It slashed at him, an inch from his throat. And all the time in his muzzy brain, he was thinking, *this is real, this is REAL and to the death no mercy,* and his rifle came up and the bayonet tore through cloth and Jones heaved with all his strength, felt a rib crack, felt the blade tear sickeningly into flesh as he pushed deeper, felt resistance slacken and the fingers on his coat loosen as the German soldier coughed blood and fell to his knees, his eyes now locked on Jones, who could only stand there and watch this man, watch him die.

Panting, Jones pried away the fingers and grimaced at their warm, sticky touch. He looked around, suddenly disengaged from his private battle. Bainbridge and another Tommy were charging away, two enemy Hun fleeing. To the right, the trench was empty. They were there. In the communications trench.

Jones moved slowly after Bainbridge, heart pounding, and rubbed dirt from his stinging eyes. He lifted his SMLE, seeing the bayonet with its indelible stain. The boards rocked beneath his boots. His mouth was drier than any desert storm.

Pausing, he fumbled and found his canteen, wet his lips, wet his throat, and could have wept at the cool relief the water provided.

He moved on. Came round a bend in the trench, watched a man emerge from a narrow connecting gulley, gun ready, his back to Jones, and he glanced towards the retreating figure of Bainbridge. Jones was just about to call out when the uniform registered, the colour leaping from the gloom. The Hun hadn't heard him, and Jones crept forward, with care, knowing he would have to plunge his bayonet into this man's back . . . he had to stab another living creature in the back . . . *in the back . . .*

His rifle was lead. His boots were filled with iron. *What I'd give for a sip of whisky, just like in the good old days,* he thought, and was almost on the German soldier, and the man must have sensed something, because he began to turn; there were shouts further down the trench but Jones's attention was focused on nothing else. With a sudden scream he thrust his rifle forward, stabbed his bayonet, but the Hun turned fast, eyes wide, rifle coming up in a gesture of defence as the two rifles smashed together, Jones's bayonet slicing a thin line up the enemy soldier's neck, and the Hun cried out, dropping his rifle, hand grasping something at his waist. In a split second, Jones realised this wasn't a common soldier; the man was an *officer,* and had a pistol—a Beholla. It came up fast; Jones drew back his rifle for another stab but it was too late . . . time slowed into a rhythmical slow beat, like the ticking of a clock. He could feel cool air around him, the drizzle, hear distant sounds of fighting, guns, the occasional mortar shell screaming through the heavens, the urgent revving of a tank's engine, and for the first time that day, Jones thought back to home, to Wales, its luscious valleys, its magnificent towering mountains, the bank where he worked with clean paper, cheques, cash, everything clean and free from mud and lice and the smell of oil and death. The whole world seemed to freeze, and he looked into the eyes of the German officer and expected to find hate and loathing and all the other things he had come to expect with his mental image of the Hun. But instead he found only pity, and panic, in those deep brown eyes. Alongside a hard-edged quality, a need to do what needed to be done. In the smallest division of a second Jones found understanding, knew they were the same, this German officer and he. They were men, they were soldiers, and it was soldiers who did the dying.

There was a *crack,* and the bullet punched up through the German's throat, exiting high and spinning off over the trench in an exhaust of blood. The body of the officer seemed to fold in on itself, and leant slowly against the trench wall, then slid quietly down into a crumpled heap.

Jones *breathed,* and glanced up. Bainbridge was pushing another magazine into his SMLE and Jones had no time for gratitude, for relief.

Bainbridge said, "Wondered where the ——ing hell you'd got to! Come on, lad. We're retreating."

"But—"

"Hun reinforcements, coming in fast! Now move!"

They climbed out of the trench, up the German ladders, could see other men of the battalion similarly withdrawing and, ducking low, began a haunt-filled sprint to

Allied lines. Occasionally, bursts of gunfire made them flinch. Nobody wanted to be shot in the back only a few yards from Allied ground.

Boots hammered on the duckboards behind them in the German communications trench, and Bainbridge and Jones could hear shouts in that harsh, guttural tongue of the Fatherland. There were several cracks and bullets whined nearby, making both Jones and Bainbridge hit the mud hard on their bellies. They crawled along, over corpses, using them as leverage, towards a huge, disintegrated tree now black with the sulphurous burns of the hell in which the Tommies fought.

Rifle shots. Screams. More of the 3rd dead, ejaculated into dreamless darkness. Jones and Bainbridge did not pause until they were past the tree and rolling down into a shell hole, cramped together, slippery fingers reloading rifles, shaking, aware of how close to death they were.

More shouts. Total confusion amidst smoke and noise. The Germans were advancing out of their trench, driving the British and French soldiers back, faces grim, rifles cracking. Heavy machine guns whined and crumps fired, shaking the earth which spat up and out in mushrooms of dirt.

A Hun passed the shell hole, crouched, creeping, and Bainbridge smashed a bullet into the man's back. Another German passed on the right, stooping to his fallen comrade, turning suddenly as realisation struck him. Jones pulled the trigger, felt the kick of the butt in his shoulder, watched the Hun throw up his arms as if to ward off the blow. The bullet took him low in the stomach and he fell into the mud, screaming at first, the scream turning to a low, drawn-out moan of pitiful pain.

Jones and Bainbridge sat there watching the soldier slowly die. He writhed on the ground, calling for somebody named Eva. His fingers clawed the mud. Bainbridge drew a knife.

"I cannot stand this!"

"Wait," said Jones. "The bullets . . ."

Bainbridge shrugged off the smaller man's grip and crawled out from the shell hole. *Always a stubborn bastard,* thought Jones, and he could see the mud soaking into Bainbridge's uniform, watched him reach the German soldier and averted eyes as Bainbridge stabbed the man swiftly through the heart.

"It's quietening down out there," said Bainbridge on his return. "I think it'll be safe for us to move soon. Our shells are pounding their trench again."

"Safe?" Jones laughed. "It'll never be safe out there. It's a stiff's paddock."

Bainbridge grinned then, his face a shadowed mask in the gloom, helmet lopsided. "Cheer up, lad! We'll soon be back in the dugout. Think of the bully and the Woodbines! Think of that hearty warm gypo stew in your belly!"

"It's bullets in my ——ing belly I'm worried about," muttered Jones.

The two Tommies checked their rifles and prepared to move. Bainbridge had been right; it was quietening down, with the Germans reluctant to advance too far after the fleeing Allies, and with fresh shells howling overhead, pounding their lines. They had regained their communications trench—and that was what mattered.

The attack had been repulsed, with many casualties.

"You ready, lad?"

Jones nodded, and the soldiers crawled on their bellies out into the rain.

———

The clouds gathered overhead. Heavy rain pounded the mud. Bainbridge and Jones struggled across the churned ground, past a stranded, twisted tank which loomed from the darkened mire like some metal dinosaur, and on, towards the warmth and fellowship of the trench.

The Hun appeared from nowhere, rearing from his hiding place behind a small, crumpled stone wall sporting barbed-wire feathers. His face was a gargoyle, his eyes wide and mad, rifle caked in mud, uniform almost unrecognisable. His rifle thundered and Jones took the bullet, was suddenly punched backwards, swallowed by water filling a shell hole. Bainbridge's reaction was instantaneous, his own rifle coming about, trigger squeezed, the barrel smoking as its missile hit the German in the throat and took another life.

The German fell back, scrabbling at the wound before slumping onto his side. His eyes glazed. Bainbridge made sure he was dead with a bayonet thrust, then turned his attention to Jones. Jumping down into the rain-filled shell hole, he wiped mud from the younger Tommy's face and tried to get a response by slapping his cheek. There was nothing. He felt for a pulse, struggling at first but finding it; it was weak and erratic. Bainbridge rummaged around and found the wound high in Jones's shoulder, and Jones's eyes flickered open. But he looked past Bainbridge, saw three looming shadows at the edge of the shell hole. They appeared as swirling ink, bulky and threatening and oozing evil.

Look! Jones wanted to scream.

Behind you!

But he could not, and gently his eyes closed again.

"You'll live, you bastard," hissed Bainbridge, unaware of the figures behind, and shouldering his rifle, he dragged Jones from the mud and hoisted the man over one shoulder with a grunt. "Now I've got to carry you!

I'll want your ——ing Woodbines for this!"

He staggered through the gloom, past the barbed wire and splintered, bullet-chipped wood.

The three looming dark figures watched him go.

Bainbridge reached the trench and called for help, allowed the scrambling, ducking Tommies to lift Jones from his aching shoulder, allowed his own weary limbs to be assisted into the dark stain of the trench.

"Third Battalion, Royal Welsh Fusiliers," he managed, coughing heavily and accepting a man's water canteen. His own had gone dry hours before, leaving his throat tender, his mouth raw.

"Is he dead?" asked a conscript.

Bainbridge fixed him with an iron stare. "Aren't we all?" he said.

WOODLAND DREAMS.
"CLEARWOOD."
6TH. OCTOBER 1903.

THE CHILD PUSHED THROUGH the tangle of woodland bracken, stooping below a low branch of ash, then scrambling up an unmarked path between two leaning, ominous oaks, ancient, gnarled, twisted, the whorls on their bark almost like faces... with dark knot eyes watching him... and then into Clearwood beyond.

He stopped, peered cautiously about himself, and coughing into a balled fist, ran a dirt-smeared hand through damp hair. Sunshine filtered in shafts from high above, but the cold chill of autumn was biting now, and the child was glad of his hat and scarf.

He was panting, chest heaving, but his eyes were bright, and he walked across the small clearing—which he had named the Clearwood. Beyond, over a wall of sprawling bramble with berries bright against dark oval leaves, lay Heartwood... and the boy's ultimate destination.

"This time," he whispered to himself, wiping sweat from his forehead and stepping forward. There was a cry, and he was startled as a chaffinch flapped from the upper reaches of the woodland with a musical rebuke.

Smiling, breathing deep, the boy approached the bracken which spread out across the sloping hillside. To each side, dense sycamore and maple had found firm footing in the clay soil, and the circle of Clearwood had only one path in . . . and one path out. But he knew the Heartwood lay up ahead, further up the shielded hill; and he knew Heartwood was the one place he had to reach.

Eyes bright, the boy reached the edge of the bracken and began negotiating the dense tangle. Leaves and twigs lay rotting on the ground, filling his nose with an aroma of damp woodland, rotting vegetation, the perfume of the ancient woods, and he pushed himself on over the bracken which snagged at jacket and trousers, as if the woods themselves were trying to pull him back.

The ground steepened and the boy's breathing became laboured, but he pulled on his gloves and they protected his hands. Thick canvas trousers protected his legs from tree bites.

He pushed on.

Up ahead, he could see it: the summit, Heartwood, populated by a dense copse of silver birch and beech . . . but the sun shone in the boy's eyes, and he squinted, breath steaming before him, limbs suddenly cold in this place.

The woods whispered, leaves rustling and bracken crunching under his shoes. But the hill had become too steep, the bracken too dense, and he slipped, shoes sliding, and something was in his mind—like a sharp pine splinter—and he felt himself being pushed back, forced back, as if the trees, whispering, chuckling, rejected his intrusion . . .

The boy shouted in surprise as his wet shoe slid, and he was sent rolling back down the hill over bracken and snagging brambles . . . He was dizzy as he came to an abrupt halt in Clearwood, cheek stinging, several coughs hacking from his chest. Putting a gloved finger to his face, he watched a spot of blood soak the fabric.

"Damn!" Frustration, shouted at the trees, which swayed, their branches speaking as if in an ancient woodland tongue.

One day, he would reach the Heartwood.

One day, he would make it past the trees, past the natural defences. It was a child's game but also a child's battle. And he *would succeed*.

In defeat, the boy turned and limped across Clearwood with twigs and leaves stuck to his jacket, a thin trickle of blood running down his cheek. It dripped, and was absorbed into the ancient soil. A connection. A bonding.

He followed the trail from Clearwood, and a bird's voice rose in song, beautiful and haunting, reminding him of his mother's voice when she sang gently at their small wooden piano . . . reminding him of his mother's words, raised suddenly in fervent, glinting anger . . .

Hark! A tumult on the mountains as of a great multitude!

Hark! An uproar of kingdoms, of nations gathering together!

The LORD of Hosts is mustering a host for battle!

They come from a distant land . . .

The boy stopped and blinked, sucking in cool woodland air. He looked around at the bright autumnal colours, absorbing the scene.

A shiver of ice ran down his spine.

What *was* that feeling?

Then he cocked his head and listened again to the bird song. It had changed from his mother's angry voice to . . .

The chaffinch?

The boy shrugged, and continued through the dense woodland with the fading song following, unable to explain to himself the absolute total belief that he was being watched by something ancient and evil.

DIARY OF ROBERT JONES.
3RD. BATTALION ROYAL WELSH FUSILIERS.
16TH. SEPTEMBER 1916.

I remember no pain. I remember Fritz, with mad eyes, and something extremely strange *flickered*. His face seemed to twist, the flesh grey and rugged, like tree bark. His limbs were crooked and angular, like the branches of a tree, and it felt like this was a revenge attack by the woods on the murder suffered by our shells. Then he was human, and his rifle thundered, and I was shot and fell into darkness where I swam like a fish in an oil ocean. I had many nightmares, where the Hun forces advanced on our trench, their faces bark, their arms and legs thudding like broken tree boughs. In one nightmare there were three huge, shadowy figures, bulky and uneven. Menace oozed from their distorted shapes as they stood, watching, as helplessly I squirmed. Finally one spoke. He, or it, said, "We're going to hunt you down."

When I awoke, Bainbridge was sitting by my bedside, head drooping as his eyes scanned the page of a book.

For a while I lay there, unable to speak, unable to question. I felt tender, as though if I moved, I would crumble into dust. Eventually, I coughed and Bainbridge looked up, his eyes bright, his mouth a crooked smile.

"Jones!"

"How about some whisky?" I'd whispered.

Bainbridge laughed loud and long, which was a surprise because I was expecting the dry rations. He slapped me on the shoulder but saw my face turn white, and he called for the nurse, who was attending to other wounded soldiers in the barracks.

Bainbridge never told me what happened out there in No Man's Land. He never told me about staggering through the mud with my dead weight across his shoulders. If I questioned him he would shrug, in that noncommittal way he does, and laugh it off. I think he was slightly embarrassed by the attention he received due to the incident. The men said he was a hero, but Bainbridge threatened to punch any man who called him such. I learned what happened from a Tommy, a man we called Soap Brush—because he was always so bloody clean! He must have spent hours scrubbing himself in his dugout.

Bainbridge saved my life. For a long time, I couldn't understand why he refused to be acknowledged as a hero. But then I realised: how could one man take praise, take the pats on the back and the medals and the bullshit, when so many of his friends were dying out there in the dark? Dying the deaths of heroes? Unrecognised, without praise, dying alone with their legs blown off or their guts spilling out over shrapnel?

Bainbridge was a hero, but he was alive, and for some reason he held this against himself. The true heroes of the war were the men whose songs went unsung, whose lives were extinguished. The ones who died alone.

PART TWO

THE RIDGE

THIEPVAL RIDGE.
27TH. SEPTEMBER 1916.

SUBSTANTIAL GAINS WERE made during recent days of fighting, with an average Allied advance of a mile and a half along the whole front. The weather worsened and slowed the advance, and this had been accompanied by German reinforcements, which brought down morale. The villages of Courcelette, Martinpuich, and Flers were successfully taken.

Jones saw active service once more on the Somme with Bainbridge by his side. His wound had been high in the shoulder, damaging muscle and chipping his clavicle, but he was soon fit for battle after a short recuperation period, in which he took as much time as possible to get to know the nurses.

Jones and Bainbridge were like brothers after the Battle of Flers-Courcelette and spent considerable time together, in the trenches, on leave, talking and laughing and experiencing life to the limit, because they both knew their lives could be taken in the blink of an eye. Jones had been lucky at Flers-Courcelette—unlike the other twenty-nine thousand allies who lost their lives.

"What are you doing after, like?" asked Bainbridge.

Jones was lying on his bunk, boots against the wall, staring at the shadows flickering on the wooden ceiling. He pulled a face. "I've not really thought about it."

"Are you going back on the drink?"

Jones smiled. "I think you've cured me of that."

"Better have, lad, or I'll knock out your teeth!"

There was a comfortable silence for a few moments.

"Do you think my father will ever forgive me?"

"What, for joining up with us normal Tommies?" said Bainbridge. "No, lad. I don't think he will. He's an officer, brass; he wanted you, with your fine private education, to follow in his bloody footsteps. A common dog like us? Ha!"

"You reckon he'll hate me forever?"

"Do you care?"

"Well, sometimes."

"Well, that's all arsapeek. Has he *ever* loved you?"

Jones smiled. "No, I don't think so. My only memories of him when I was a kid are of him shouting, that loud commanding voice—a bit like yours. And I remember his silly drooping moustache. It made him look like a clown. To a kid's eyes, anyway."

Bainbridge, who was carefully sewing a tear in his coat, looked up, his eyes squinting in the candlelight. "How's the shoulder?"

"Tender. I'm a disgrace to them. My family, I mean; aren't I?"

"Yes."

"Your honesty overwhelms me."

Bainbridge grunted, and snapped the cotton thread with his teeth. "Any lad who rolls around in the gutter after filling his gut with whisky is bound to disgrace his family, all right? By its very nature, whisky is a dirty drink that makes men do things they wouldn't otherwise do."

"But most men drink whisky," said Jones. "It's normal to want a sip."

"Night after night? Bottle after bottle?"

"Well . . ."

"And there were the women, as well, you ——ing bumbrusher. And the gambling. You'll still have to face that Tyson when you get back to Blighty."

"You sure delivered his men a good thrashing," laughed Jones, and Bainbridge smiled, happy to see the young Tommy in such good humour. "How many teeth did you knock out?"

"It was just a shame you weren't awake to see it," said Bainbridge, scowling a little.

"Well, you did okay in that fight on your own!"

"No thanks to you. But seriously, Jones, that Tyson is a nasty piece of work. He'll want his money the minute your boots touch the cobbles. And he'll come with weapons next time, and a full divvy of men."

Jones sighed. "That's why I'm here, ain't it? To earn a pretty penny so I can pay off those nasty debts that embarrass my mother so."

"Yeah. And to save your scrawny neck." Bainbridge packed away his sewing case carefully and rubbed his eyes. "Time for sleep, mate. Another day, another battle."

"Another battle," whispered Jones, and stared at the ceiling.

———

The morning was clear and fresh. A breeze blew in from the east, and the sun was hidden behind high, white clouds. Bainbridge had a tin of toffee which he shared with a small group of privates, and as they readied themselves at the base of the trench ladders, he shouted over to Jones, "Save me some of your cigarettes, lad."

Jones gave a mock salute and Bainbridge laughed. "It's a fine day to be alive, ain't it? A bloody fine day." He stuffed his mouth full of toffee, grinned, cast away the tin, and as the whistles sounded, scrambled up the ladder and over the bags with the rest of the infantry.

They advanced on Thiepval Ridge. Bullets cracked and roared, mortar shells exploded, and men went down screaming with shrapnel in their eyes. They were running, crouching low, and an explosion ahead separated Bainbridge and Jones. Dropping into a trench with another six lads, Jones jabbed his bayonet through a Hun's heart, stepped over the body, saw a pistol come up—but one of the lads behind fired his rifle over Jones's shoulder. The crack deafened him. The officer was punched from his feet, splashing onto the sodden duckboards.

Suddenly, Jones felt a shiver crawl down his spine. He glanced left. There, in the midst of the battlefield, were three large, bulky, swirling-ink figures. They were watching him. His mouth fell open, limbs suddenly freezing, fear itching his scalp. Slowly, one of the figures lifted its arm and pointed at him. The limb looked like bark, fingers like twigs. Jones blinked. The figures flickered. They *looked* like Hun but were not. Their faces were more elongated, seemed to have muzzles like dogs, with long, curved yellow fangs.

Jones blinked again, and they were gone.

"Go on!" screamed an officer, pushing him. "What you standing there for?"

Jones stumbled forward clutching his Lee-Enfield.

They charged along the trench. More Tommies came over the side, and ahead, the Hun were fleeing. A Tommy called Jackson fired his rifle, shooting a Hun in the back. He glanced at Jones with mean eyes.

"He would have done the same to us," he said.

Jones nodded, but all he could picture were the yellow fangs.

———————

By nightfall, it was over. The ridge had been taken, despite ferocious fighting by the German defenders, and the lines advanced. Bainbridge, cheek scorched from a rifle blast, roamed the trenches looking for Jones, calling out the Tommy's name and asking privates after the soldier's whereabouts.

With a sinking feeling in the pit of his stomach, he finally walked to the hospital. Bainbridge knew it should have been the first place to check, but he hated hospitals, their chemical stink, their moaning inmates, and he knew that by visiting the hospital first, it could have almost been an omen—an admission to himself that Jones had been wounded—possibly killed—and so, when he finally dragged his boots through the mud and appeared in the wooden building's doorway, he found himself relieved to see Jones sitting up in a chair, thigh heavily bandaged, the bandage soaked with blood, his face tightly drawn and teeth gritted in pain.

"I always seem to find you here, lad," said Bainbridge, grinning, pulling up another chair, and trying to blank out the sounds of dying men in nearby beds, and even on the floor.

"That's because I'm always ——ing wounded," snapped Jones. "A ——ing bayonet wound to the leg! They say it's not serious, but it hurts like holy ——. I see you didn't get wounded! What's wrong with you? Touched by God or something?"

"Hmm. You're lucky you didn't throw a seven. Maybe if you'd stuck with me, some of my angelic luck would have rubbed off," beamed Bainbridge, pulling out a packet of Woodbines and tapping one free.

"No coffin nails in here!" snapped a passing nurse, her face stern.

"Bloody hell, is nothing sacred?" growled Bainbridge.

For a few minutes they sat in silence, Bainbridge playing with his unlit cigarette and studying the heavy curtains behind the bed. In the distance a crump exploded; the noise was strange, muffled, alien to this hospital environment and quiet groaning and dimmed lights.

"I've had enough," said Jones, eventually, wincing and gripping the muscle around the bandage.

"What, of your leg? You're damn lucky they ain't cutting it off!"

"No, of the war. The killing. I preferred my life before.

The taste of whisky sweet on my tongue, a long-legged blonde sweet in my bed . . ."

Bainbridge nodded, feeling the mood sour beyond even his eternal optimism.

"Smoky died today," said Jones.

"Smoky! Damn, he was a fine lad. How did that ——ing happen?"

"Shrapnel. Caught the full shrap from a stick grenade. I was behind the poor chap and he shielded me from the blast. But it could have easily been me, Bainbridge. Do you see? Then, no more women for Jones, no more whisky and willing, open legs."

"You're not to bloody give up now, soldier," snapped Bainbridge. "You hear me? I've heard men talking in the trenches, their mouths full of gypo. They've given up, half of them. They only go over the bloody top because they're scared of being shot as bloody deserters by some ——ing brass hat . . . and that's no way to go. You can't fight when you're absorbed in defeat, Jones. You can't take an enemy trench when you're wondering if the next bullet is meant for you!"

"I know that." Jones gritted his teeth again. "But this is my second injury in battle. I'm wondering if the third will be my last, understand?"

"And if you think like that, then you will get stiffed," said Bainbridge, his voice cold. "There's no room for cowardice on the front lines; you know it and I know it. Don't lose your balls now, Jones. Don't lose them, like those other blokes."

Jones reached out, his hand gripping Bainbridge's shoulder with passion. "I'm a soldier, Charles. I've been over the bags, what? Seven times? I'm not a stay-at-homer, I'm no coward, and I still have my mind. I'm alive. But I want to stay that ——ing way, I want to go home, marry, and have children. I want to watch my children grow up into healthy men, women! I want to grow old before a roaring fire and drink brandy every night and go back to work in the bank. I was a clerk before this, you know?"

"You've told me," said Bainbridge.

"Well, now I understand. I'm a *clerk*. I'm an unwilling soldier—yeah, so I had thoughts of grandeur, heroism, I wanted to clear my name, to be rid of the image of drink and women and gambling... but I was wrong to join up. I was running away, running away from responsibility and debt. There's no heroism here, Bainbridge. You are different, though, Charlie, it's as if you... as if you ——ing *enjoy* going over the top! Christ, you don't have any fear. You charge in there with your Enfield thundering and you're a ——ing hero."

"I'm not a—"

"Don't say it. I know; I've heard your speeches before.

55

But the men, they look up to you. You'll be promoted; mark my words. The brass are watching you. But this life isn't for me, and that's just a fact." Seeing the look of sadness on Bainbridge's face, Jones continued, "Don't worry; I'm not about to desert." He gave a bitter laugh. "I'll serve out my time, even if it means going back to Blighty in a wooden box. But don't preach to me about cowardice, because out here in the trenches there's no such ——ing thing . . . if a man is scared, he's got every right to be scared. Look around you! Fear isn't cowardice, Charlie. Any man who's been over the bags and through the stiff's paddock simply *can't* be a coward."

They were interrupted by a nurse on her observation round, and she took Jones's temperature, pulse, and blood pressure and Bainbridge stood and moved to the window, looking out, still playing with his cigarette. When she spoke, her voice was soft, husky. Jones looked into her eyes, admiring her femininity. It had been a long time since he had been close to a woman. Far too long. But she turned briskly away, moved to the next patient, and performed her duties. She did not have time for soft words when men were dying around her.

"Thank you, nurse," whispered Jones, and put his head in his hands.

———————

The hospital was sometimes quiet, but not tonight. Men moaned and whimpered, some cried out. The building was not far enough behind the lines to kill the sound of the crumps, the guns, the whizz-bangs.

Distant, muffled explosions kept Jones awake long into the early hours.

When he finally fell asleep, the smell of disinfectant strong in his nostrils, he dreamt of the war and No Man's Land and a forest of blackened trees:

He was in the trench, alone. He looked left and right, across the muddied, stained duckboards, eyes searching hopefully for some other soldier, some friend to accompany him over the wire. But there was nobody there. He was alone, and frightened.

"I am not a coward," he told himself. "I will do my duty for King and Country!" But the words seemed hollow in own ears, weak and false and filled with a sadness that went down to his marrow.

The whistles sounded, ghostly echoes from some eerie otherworld, and Jones gripped his rifle tight, clambered up the ladder, over the wire, into No Man's Land and the enveloping darkness beyond.

Silent, black, burnt trees surrounded him—and ate him whole.

Turning to look back, Jones could no longer see the trench. It had gone. There was no way back home.

Guns roared in the distance, mortar shells exploded, kicking up great mushrooms of earth and shattering broken trees, which cracked and fell. Jones ran, advancing on the enemy lines, and tanks suddenly loomed out of the darkness around him, their stinking, choking fumes making him cough and choke and retch, and he was in their centre, they were advancing together across the field of the slain, and the tanks' heavy iron tracks crushed twisted corpses and blackened sulphur trees down into the mud, their great iron eyes merciless in this, their terrible onslaught. Jones knew this was only a dream, strained from his fevered imagination, tortured from his soul by the horrors he had witnessed . . . but even in dreams friends can die, in dreams it is a thousand times worse, in dreams they can die over and over and over again with no hope of peace or redemption . . .

Jones ran on, left behind the foul tanks that were floundering, engines sparking and grinding, unholy weapons of destruction.

He was near the centre of the battlefield, where the corpses were thickest. Flies were black in the air, the stink heavy in his throat, and he fell to his knees beside a stump of blackened deadwood, his rifle forgotten as he heaved and retched, vomit splashing his clean uniform, staining him with its impurity.

When the pain passed, he glanced up, saw a corpse nearby, and it was Bainbridge. Jones froze in shock.

The sounds of battle froze also.

A complete silence filled the air, the scene, the world.

For a moment, it appeared Bainbridge had been carved from wood, ebony timber, but then the image came into focus and Jones could see his friend's eyes had been pecked out by the crows. He looked strangely at peace despite this mutilation. His rifle was grasped in unmoving, blood-speckled hands, dry holes in his chest where bullets had ripped away his life. He appeared peaceful in death. A statue. Staring into the tombworld with his ruined eye sockets.

"Why?" asked Jones, dragging himself to his feet. "Why us?"

The guns started again, making Jones flinch. Machine guns in the darkness, their hollow cackles filling the air and mocking Jones with an eternal metal song. And he watched, with open mouth, as a line of Hun climbed from their trench and advanced towards him, grey hands grasping rifles, grey faces twisting and contorting, as if their very flesh were hot wax, continually melting and shifting. They had no features, these blank German soldiers, and their limbs were twitching, snapping backwards and forward, their knees bending the wrong way, as they broke into twisted, deformed runs, and Jones fell to his knees, tears streaming down his face, screaming as their rifles lifted and, as one, opened fire on him . . .

Jones awoke in the early hours of the morning, shivering violently. He reached down, wincing at the pain in his injured leg and dragging the blankets back up over his body. He lay there waiting to warm up, and thought back to his dream, the short glimpses of nightmare he could still remember. He could remember the guns, even as he was suddenly aware that the guns, *real guns,* were firing now, distant, muffled. It was a night offensive, and Jones wondered if Bainbridge had gone over the bags.

He shuddered.

Placing his hands together, something Jones had not done since he was a child, he whispered, "Please, Lord, keep Charles Bainbridge safe from the bullets and the shrapnel, bring him back to the trench alive. Let the trees watch over him. Amen."

He closed his eyes and allowed sleep to gently take him.

Again, his dreams were haunted.

WOODLAND DREAMS.
23RD. OCTOBER 1903.

WHEN THE CHILD returned home, his mother scolded him for his dirty clothes and cut cheek, had warned him to keep away from the woods, especially the ancient Devil Wood to the east. She made him promise to play in safer realms.

The following weekend, after he had been put to bed and the sun was dropping behind the mountains, bathing them in crimson, he had pushed open the sash window and climbed down the thick ivy which covered that side of the cottage. He paused by an open window, listening as his father muttered to himself as he read from a large, battered Bible. Through cool air, he walked down green lanes lined with trees, down narrow winding roads, quiet and beautiful. Reaching the edge of the woods, he eyed the trees with suspicion. Here, they seemed normal. Oak, ash, and sycamore, mixed in with towering pine, upper branches swaying gently, leaves rustling. An idyllic scene.

But as the boy stepped through this outer barrier, picking his way carefully through the undergrowth, once more he felt he was being watched. And as the sun finally fell, and moonlight bathed the woods, everything seemed outlined in silver. It was utterly beautiful, and utterly terrifying.

What had his mother called it? The Devil Wood. He shivered. Why would she call it that?

With rising fear but a grim determination, the boy found the narrow path with some difficulty and began his journey through fields of twisted oak. As he progressed, so the trees became older, larger, more twisted, winding in upon themselves like great deformed beasts. It grew yet darker, the canopy blocking out most of the moonlight, and the gloom frightened the boy, for he had never travelled in the woods at night. Everything was louder, had more clarity. The crunch of his shoes. The sounds of small animals foraging. The creak of ancient boughs.

Halting in a clearing, the boy crouched and listened. To his left a creature, probably a badger or fox, was snuffling in the leaf carpet.

Up ahead was totally silent. The silence of the tomb.

Again came the unnerving feeling he was being watched. Not by an animal, or even necessarily a person; but *something* that lived in the woods. Something terrible.

It began to rain, and water dripped from the leaves as the boy finally reached Clearwood. He moved swiftly to the sprawling bracken and again attempted the climb, this time with more care, taking the time to find stronger roots and testing his weight before trusting them with his violent tugs.

He progressed.

The hill was steep, and the boy had seen it from the distance where it rose, a carpeted bump in the fabric of the land. His father called it Hunter's Hill, but the boy did not know why, and found his father much too daunting to approach with such questions.

The call of a tawny owl made the boy jump, and he paused, then concentrated more on his slow climb until he finally stood, triumphant, cheeks glowing, sweat damping his back—a victor over the bracken defences!

The land now levelled, and the boy wandered between stands of silver birch, looking about him in awe.

Drifting clouds obscured the moon's light for a while, and the boy waited in the damp gloom, then moved forward at a reduced pace. When finally the moon reappeared, he found himself beside a wound in the ground; and looking left and right, he realised it was a long, winding trench. It connected to a high cliff. Impassable. Below him, filling the trench, was an insane tangle of deadwood, which must have accumulated over decades. Instinctively, he knew he had to cross.

"Sharpwood," said the boy out loud, naming that part of the woodland, letting the trees know of his presence, his intrusion, his acceptance of their rules. He could feel eyes on him. And a word came to him.

Skogsgrå.

And he knew it was she who watched.

The ground was thickly carpeted with leaves and twigs, and past Sharpwood the hillside was obscured by massive conifers and the odd towering beech, dark branches spread to the sky.

The boy looked on. The Sharpwood appeared dangerous, especially in darkness, and he trembled, unsure.

Come. Come to me.

The words drifted to him, like the hissing of leaves, the patter of rain, the sounds of nature forming words he could understand.

Cross Sharpwood. You can do it.

Beyond lies the truth.

Beyond lies a gift.

Beyond lie all your future dreams . . .

Feeling almost hypnotised, the boy moved to the edge of the deadly pit filled with natural sharpened stakes. He stood there in the rain, face pale, and coughed a few times, wiped his lips, and stepped out onto the first treacherous branch, his arms spread wide to balance himself, and the branch creaked, and from somewhere deep in the trench there came a *crack*. The boy shuddered.

Behind him, in the rain, like ghosts detaching from smoke, there emerged a figure, naked, skin grey and corrugated like the bark of a tree.

The Skogsgrå.

By her side emerged a second figure, with grey skin and hair like black fungus.

The Huldra.

Their fingers curled together, like trees roots entwining, and they watched the boy struggling to cross the trap.

BATTLE OF THE TRANSLOY RIDGES.
3RD. OCTOBER 1916.

BAINBRIDGE SAT ON his bunk, Lee-Enfield on his lap, cleaning and oiling parts. His boots were well-shined, uniform recently patched where a Hun knife had sliced close to his ribs, but now it was pressed and clean.

Jones ducked through the heavy curtain, smiled a greeting at Bainbridge and removed a canvas satchel from his shoulder which he hung against the wooden boards. Taking a tin cup, he filled it with water, sipped a little, and said, "You having fun?"

"You look like you've bloody drowned, like," said Bainbridge, as Jones put the tin cup down, removed his helmet, and threw it onto his bunk. Water ran in rivulets down the metal dome and soaked into his blankets.

"I feel as if I've drowned!" muttered Jones, moving to a small mirror the men used for shaving, to survey his damp features. "Have you got a towel there?"

Bainbridge threw Jones a coarse towel, and the Tommy rubbed his face and hair, and then slung the towel over one shoulder.

"If this rain keeps up, they might postpone the off,"

said Jones, combing his hair in front of the small mirror and rubbing his eyes. He yawned. "I'm buggered worse than any body snatcher in the field. I could do with more sleep!"

Bainbridge said nothing and continued to oil his rifle. When he'd finished, he stretched back on his bunk, watching the flickering candle which had been stuck to an upside-down tin of Ovaltine by its own wax. "We haven't got time for sleep now," he said finally, voice soft, eyes transfixed. "It's our turn. The guns have been roaring for two days, but now it's our turn."

Jones said nothing. Both men were melancholy, awaiting the dawn light and the push. The French offensive was drawing out, the heavy rain making battle difficult, if not impossible. Countless men and horses had drowned in the mud, thousands of lives been lost to the chattering mockery of guns and mortar bombs. All sense of optimism at Marshal Joffre's promises of a speedy offensive from Maricourt to Gommecourt had faded. The initial benefit of the tanks under Haig had been heavily criticised, and the war effort was losing momentum, losing morale, losing ——ing men. Joffre's apparent indifference to heavy French losses on the Somme, combined with the tactical errors of Rawlinson, did nothing to boost the flagging morale of soldiers on the allied front lines. And somehow, Bainbridge and Jones found themselves ready to go over the bags once more.

"The mud is endless," said Jones, checking his gas mask. He waved the mask at Bainbridge. "Have you checked yours? The Hun have been using phosgene again . . . I saw Jock in the mess hall and he told me how Smiler went over on the first. The gas got him. Choked to death on his own ——ing vomit."

Bainbridge nodded but said nothing. His forehead was creased, as if in deep thought, and finally he pushed aside his rifle, swung his legs from his bunk, and pulled on his boots. "Come on. The sarge will be calling us out soon."

"Yes."

"And I need a smoko."

Bainbridge laced up his boots, put on his helmet, checked his canteen, pulled on his waterproofs, and headed out into the darkness.

Jones rubbed his jaw, feeling weariness settle across his shoulders like snow. *Will this ever be over? Will it ever end? Is tonight the night I'm brought back by the body snatchers? Shit.*

He sighed, picked up his helmet, and extinguished the candle.

For a second—a split second—the darkness kicked him back to his childhood. Running, shoes slipping, through the woods. Chased. Chased by evil . . . but then it was gone, and he was pushing aside the mouldy curtain and grunting as he heaved himself into the trench.

Bainbridge was there, dripping under the downpour, sharing a story with another Tommy. It appeared four men had been beaten quite badly by the company sergeant major because one of the men caught measles, and in an attempt to earn themselves a ride back to England, his mates had shared his bunk for several nights in the hope of contracting the disease. The CSM caught them and gave them his own discipline.

Now the CSM was up in front of Brigadier Isaacs, a Welsh officer who was not renowned for his leniency, compassion, nor sense of humour. Bainbridge was laughing out loud as this story was relayed, and Jones looked on through the rain, seeing a large man, a large friend, standing bulky and *glowing* as the dawn approached, damp wood, sandbags, and barbed wire behind, his bayonet a flash of silver, face now smudged with dirt despite his cleanliness only moments earlier.

"May God go with us," said Jones, looking up into eerie, rain-filled heavens. He straightened his helmet, wiggled toes in damp boots, and mentally prepared himself for battle.

Over the bags and into No Man's Land. The fighting was fierce, the covering machine gun fire roaring from thirty Lewises and Vickers set at strategically placed positions; but still the advancing battalions were cut down, bullets hissing through the rain and punching through waterproofs, kicking men onto their backs, exploding their blood across the soil of France.

Jones and Bainbridge ducked heads as a mortar shell exploded nearby, and shrapnel whirred overhead. Bainbridge staggered up, his temper fired, his anger overcoming him.

"Down!" screamed Jones, but Bainbridge charged forward, discharging his rifle into the gloom as hisses kicked up bullet splashes at his feet and Jones was charging after his friend as more crumps howled through the sky, and men were screaming in the mud and the ground rocked with the force of pounding explosions.

Bainbridge went down with a bullet in the leg, and groaning, he rolled onto his back, stared at the sky, and opened his mouth as a sudden thirst overcame him.

Jones slumped down next to the large Tommy, mud splashing his face and making him blink at the gritty, slimy texture. It tasted foul on his lips, and he pulled out his canteen but could find nowhere clean or dry to wipe the top, and so had to drink mud with his water. *So that's what they call Anzac Soup,* he thought, and nearly retched.

Bainbridge was moaning, a low, pain-filled sound. Jones forced a little water down Bainbridge's throat and hissed, "I'm going to have a look at the wound . . . now, don't cry out."

"Yeah, right, well, I ain't no ——ing girl."

Gunfire rattled in the distance. A crump howled overhead.

Jones crawled his way down until he was level with Bainbridge's leg, and delicately, he took hold of a flap of cotton and eased it from the mangled flesh. The wound was deep and blood oozed from split skin. The flesh surrounding the bullet hole was scorched, black, and blood-stained cloth nestled inside the wound. Jones cursed and resisted the temptation to poke inside. He could see the bullet needed to come out—but not here!

He crawled back so he could speak. He smiled. "It isn't bad. Bainbridge . . . Bainbridge!"

"Uh . . . what?"

"It isn't bad. Look . . . remember that time you carried me back? Remember? And I had to give you all my Woodbines? You bastard. Well, it's my turn now, only I can't carry you . . . there's too much gunfire and you're a fat ——er. I'm going to crawl, and drag you behind me. Are you listening to me?"

"I'm . . . tired."

"No, Bainbridge!" He slapped the Tommy's face.

"You can't go to sleep; we've got to get you back to the trench or to the stretcher bearers . . . Now, you've got to help me, okay?"

Bainbridge nodded, coughed, and gritted his teeth in pain. "It hurts like hell."

"I know. But work with me. Come on, you tough bastard."

Jones took a firm hold on his friend's collar and started to struggle through the mud as bullets whined around him. Corpses were the hardest to overcome, and Jones soon learned to crawl around them as his muscles screamed and Bainbridge became heavier by the second.

More crumps hissed through the rain, and Jones forced Bainbridge's face into the mud as the ground shook and hot metal scythed the field.

"That was close," murmured Bainbridge.

"Are you okay there, chaps?"

Jones looked up, spied a lance corporal whose face shone white in the gloom; he was a young man, younger than Jones, and had cut himself on the chin shaving. He crouched beside the Tommies.

"He's been hit," said Jones.

"We're taking the ridge; we need all the men who can fight and we need them now," said the lance corporal. "There are body snatchers nearby; they'll find your friend . . ."

"He'll die out here," hissed Jones, but further words were cut off as a crump appeared from the sky, wailing as if in pain... The lance corporal hit the ground as shrapnel exploded in a burst of flames, and Jones screamed as the explosion burned his skin, punching him sideways, and the mud was cool beneath him. He tried to squirm into it, to cover himself, to hide himself from the enemy like a kid under a blanket. But it was incredibly difficult to move, incredibly difficult to do anything...

He opened his eyes, which seemed to have been glued.

The lance corporal was sitting before him, tongue hanging out like a panting dog. Jones started to speak, until he realised the man was dead. He searched the soldier's body with his eyes, and he could see the massive wound, across his abdomen, where his bowels had spilled out and steamed in the rain.

"No," he whispered, and then realised he, also, had been hit. Jones had taken shrapnel from the bomb. He wanted desperately to check himself for wounds, check for gaping holes spilling blood to the dirt-strewn earth... but he could not. He had to get Bainbridge back. ——. Had to get *himself* back...

He paused. Analysed himself. Could feel pain in his left side and across the left side of his face.

A bullet whined past his ear, close to his cheek, making him jump. With the jump, he felt blood pulse down his flesh beneath his shirt. "Shit. Don't let us die," he whispered. "Please don't let us die out here!"

He grabbed Bainbridge, started tugging at him, dragging him along. But the bastard was heavier than a dead donkey!

"Charlie! Charlie!"

He glanced back. Bainbridge was unconscious.

"——."

Jones tried to pull Bainbridge again, but he could not. His strength fled him, and he slumped back, so his face was next to his friend's.

He couldn't move. Couldn't think!

More bullets whined and spat. There were screams nearby, somebody dying in the mud.

Jones heard boots, mud slopping, and the click of a cocking rifle. Help! Help had arrived! The stretcher bearers were here, ready to cart Bainbridge and himself back to the trench!

Jones twisted his head round. To see a Hun, crouched on one knee, staring at him . . . only it wasn't a Hun—it was a *creature*, a *monster*, huge and bulky, wearing a German uniform. The face was grey, ridged, bark run through with corrugations of black. There was a long muzzle with yellow fangs, from which smoke oozed. Dark eyes glittered with an alien intelligence. And yet, and *yet* he—it—wore the uniform of a German soldier, large, bulky, and a helmet sat on the beast's head—and the steel merged with bubbling, hot-wax flesh . . .

With fingers like bark, the creature lifted the rifle and sighted at Jones.

"What are you?" he growled, "What the —— are you?"

The rifle wavered, and lowered a little. Those glittering eyes bore into Jones and he wanted to puke.

"You do not remember, little man?" The voice was incredibly coarse and completely non-human. No human larynx could create such guttural sounds.

"*Remember*? What the hell does that mean?"

The creature shrugged, with bony, ridged shoulders. The face contorted, into what might have been humour or might have been pain. "We have been watching you, Robert Jones. You and your . . . *ilk*." The muzzle moved like a human mouth, twisting and gnashing. Drool spooled from the twisted fangs. "We are *walriders*." It grinned. "Welcome to our world."

"I . . . don't understand!"

"We want your eyes and your soul. Prepare to die."

The rifle lifted once more, and Jones saw the twig-finger tighten on the trigger.

"No!" he screamed as his eyes clicked shut.

He was in the woods. Around him, trees were black and lifeless, as if a massive fire had raged through, decimating the trunks, scorching all life from the woods. Jones sat up and looked about. His brow creased in confusion. And then he saw the lance corporal, with his protruding tongue and abdomen ripped open by shrapnel. Bowels were writhing with maggots. The tongue and eyes were covered in ants.

The body was ten days old and rotting. The stink of it offended Jones's nostrils, and suddenly he felt laughter well up his throat, disgorged from his spinning brain, because, well, shit. Because he must be dead.

He climbed to his feet and screamed into the trees, "Come on, then! What the —— happens next?"

But only silence flowed back, like freezing air over a glacier.

Jones fell to his knees. And he remembered.

Remembered the Skogsgrå. Remembered the Huldra.

Remembered the trees burning. The world burning!

And he lowered his head and wept.

_____

When Jones awoke, it was to confusion. His eyes were nailed shut, but he could hear and smell things that did not fit. A jigsaw puzzle with himself in the middle. Around him were people—unknown people—and he had placed the wrong pieces in the wrong holes, and it just did not mesh.

He coughed, winced as a dull throb ached in his back and his side, and he tried to reach behind himself, could feel something bulky *behind,* but the pain when he moved his arms was too intense, and so he just lay there, panting.

A scream echoed, followed by shouts. Jones could smell blood, and rain, and mud, and that offensive medical smell which always accompanies hospitals: metallic, acidic, but welcome as a sign of life and civilisation.

He tried to open his eyes. He coughed again. Felt a warm hand on his brow, felt something glass slipped into his mouth.

"Where . . ." he tried.

"Shh. Rest. You're safe now." The man's voice was soothing and Jones lost himself once more in the drifting darkness, amidst the trees and the fire and the burning world, and didn't remember anything until a shout of pain awoke him much, much later.

———————

This time, Jones was more aware of his surroundings. He could hear groaning to his left. That medical stink still filled his nostrils and a voice said, "He's awake."

Jones opened his eyes.

It was night, Jones assumed, because the curtains had been drawn and bare bulbs lit the field hospital. A nurse approached, her face weary, her eyes dark-ringed and heavy. She forced a smile and took Jones's blood pressure and pulse. He watched her all the time, sympathising with this poor creature who had to attend the mangled remains of men brought in off the battlefield. She didn't deserve the horrors she was forced to endure.

He was tired, but an incredible thirst overtook. "Water?" he croaked.

"Just a little," said the nurse, smiling with lead-lined eyes. "The doctor will operate soon and you've to keep off fluids."

She allowed Jones a sip.

"Bainbridge?" he asked.

"Pardon?"

"A . . . a soldier. My friend. Bainbridge."

"I'm sorry," said the nurse. "There have been many

wounded during the last few days. Some are here; some have been shipped to hospitals further behind the front. I don't know of any man called Bainbridge."

Jones nodded and felt himself slipping into sleep. He remembered being moved on a trolley towards a fiery red pain in his dreams. But that was all, and he slept for a very long time in the tombworld.

DIARY OF ROBERT JONES.
3RD. BATTALION ROYAL WELSH FUSILIERS.
20TH. OCTOBER 1916.

It was good of the sergeant to bring over my diary, but the sad thing is there are many blank pages which I just cannot fill. The memories are not there. My mind is blank. Except for those who . . . hunt.

Getting shrapnel in the back and ribs does that to a man. Apparently, it was touch and go for a while as I hovered near the brink of death.

I do remember one thing, though.

The German soldier, the *walrider*, with the grey face and muzzle and limbs carved like branches. I remember him lifting his rifle. And yet . . . yet I am still here. What happened? Why did it not shoot?

Part of me is terrified. And yet part of me is filled with a furious anger.

These creatures which appear in my dreams (in reality) seem to be hunting me. And despite my terror, I know deep down in my soul that one day I must face them. Face them, and kill them. Or die.

I've a lovely pack of bandaging on my torso now, and I'm informed I will have a lot of scarring. But then, what's a scar if a man still has life? At least the Somme for me is over, and my miserable damp world in the trenches soon to be forgotten. Well. Never truly forgotten.

Bainbridge lived, that tough cockroach! I've been told I might see the old grumpy bastard tomorrow when we're both being shipped back to Blighty. I'm sure his wife, Helen, will be pleased to see him alive. He doesn't really talk about her much, and I suppose it's because he's scared to death of never seeing her again. It's his protection mechanism.

If I was a married man, then I'm sure I'd talk about my wife. I suppose I never got around to marriage, the whisky probably scaring them all off... maybe now though, a "hero" of the war, maybe now I'll be able to settle down and have children.

Yes. An incentive. Something to keep me off the drink and gambling, something to make me face up to myself and larger, more important responsibilities. Maybe this experience will earn me a little respect in the bank... that's if the bastards still have the job open for me. Do I really care? No. —— the bank. I'm not sure I can sit on my backside all day any longer. Not after what I've been through; not after the horrors I've seen.

I wonder how my old friend George is getting on? I hope I'll see him again soon. However, the poor sod will be conscription age before long and might get drafted into this hell hole. No wonder they don't tell you what it's like back home! Only a madman, or a man with nothing to live for, would voluntarily sign up. Who's for the game, the biggest that's played? Yeah. How ———ing tragic. How deeply tragic.

After my meal, I had a long talk with the nurse who tended me and about fifty other poor bastards who took metal at Transloy. She is extremely beautiful. Her name is Sarah, and she has the most dazzling, beaming smile, and a laugh that can melt a man's heart from a hundred yards.

The best thing about Sarah is she doesn't question me about life in the trenches, about the war. She is intelligent, and radiant, and she held my hand tonight and read to me. Jules Verne, *Journey to the Centre of the Earth*. A fabulous hardback edition with illustrations by Édouard Riou.

It's an amazing adventure story.

I wanted to tell her about the monsters that hunt me. But I could not.

I think, for the first time, I'm in love.

I hope I will see her again.

DIARY OF ROBERT JONES.
3RD. BATTALION ROYAL WELSH FUSILIERS.
21ST. OCTOBER 1916.

I saw Bainbridge today. After breakfast, Sarah helped me into a wheelchair (with much wincing, I can tell you) and she wheeled me across the compound. There he was, smoking a Woodbine, sat out under a canvas shelter reserved for smokers. Smoking is outlawed in the field hospitals, which is a sad irony because a coffin nail is the one joy a man can have in these places of hell, except for the bully. That is, of course, unless you can get hold of some whisky, but now whisky's more valuable than gold in the trenches.

I talked with Bainbridge, and we had a laugh. He showed me his bandaged thigh, which had luckily not become infected with gangrene, or he would have lost the leg. The German bullet had shattered part of his femur and he had difficulty walking, but the doctor said Bainbridge would recover full mobility after a few months. That made the ——er happy.

Bainbridge showed me a pistol he'd stolen—what we call a souvy, a battlefield souvenir. The body snatchers brought in a Tommy who was worse for wear after scuffling with a Hun. In his hand he held a pistol ripped from the Hun's holster, and Bainbridge's eagle eyes spotted the weapon, and he'd performed his own midnight reconnaissance of the hospital, picking up the Beholla en route. Bainbridge was proud of the gun, showed it to me as a trophy. It was a 7.65mm automatic and took a seven-round magazine. The only problem was it had no bullets, but Bainbridge didn't let this damp his enthusiasm. He spoke of how poetic it would be to snuff out Germans with their own guns. Poetic, and tragic, I said.

I think Bainbridge has lost it. We've both seen the dark side of war, and now we're going home, we're just glad to be alive.

One change in Bainbridge's talk now is his lack of heroic bullshit. He no longer rants about a need for fighting, a desire to kill the enemies of our king. He is a changed man. Only time will tell *how* changed.

Just before I left, Bainbridge handed me a couple of Woodbines when Sarah wasn't looking. I hid them down my chat bags. Bainbridge then looked deep into my eyes. "Do you still have the nightmares?" he asked, and although I knew damned well what he was talking about, I told him no. Sometimes, lies are the only option.

I left then, worried by his words. I knew I'd spoken to him of nightmares, of being lost in a forest surrounded by choking tanks and blackened trees, an unholy place not dissimilar to No Man's Land.

There had been something in his eyes. A question.

It was as if he *knew* about the Skogsgrå and the Huldra. About my bad dreams. About the fire burning down the world.

But I blanked it all. I just wanted out of France.

I wanted to go home.

———————

Before I left, Sarah gave me her home address back in England. I said I would look her up, and she kissed me on the cheek. It was the best kiss I've ever had, and I can still smell the starch of her uniform, and her faint musky scent which made my heart race. I truly hope I see her again. I hope she wants to see *me* again. After all, hundreds of men pass through the hospital every week, and after a while, one man must seem very much the same as any other.

———————

The engines echo deep in the bowels of the collier as I write this, and the English Channel is incredibly rough. "Choppy" is the word the Captain used. Yes. Right, mate.

I've never been a seafarer, and feel sicker than I've ever done before. *Choppy.*

I hope the journey will be over soon. I will try and get some sleep after writing, like that snoring bugger Bainbridge on the opposite bunk. I don't know how he got us a cabin together; I think he bribed some official with cigars. But I don't bloody know where he got the cigars!

The name of our ship is the *Prince Charles,* once a coal transporter but now used as a Q-ship with concealed guns and torpedoes for sinking U-boats. One of the crew, a sailor called Evans, told me this particular Q-ship sank U-36 off the Orkneys in 1915, something he was apparently very proud of.

Somehow, I don't know how, Bainbridge has managed to get covered in coal dust. I can see his smudged face through the darkness as he snores like a bloody pig.

I hope I can sleep.

I hope the nightmares don't return.

———

I met Sarah by the bus stop on Castle Terrace in Dolwyddelan. The sun was shining, and as we walked towards Church Street, where I was boarding, she reached over and held my hand. With heart racing, I squeezed her fingers, and looked at her, and she smiled, we smiled, and stared at one another like children.

"You have a castle here, don't you?"

"Yeah, built in 1210 by Llywelyn, ruler of North Wales. I used to play there as a child. And . . . in the surrounding woods."

"It sounds beautiful." She looked around. "This is an amazing place!"

"We can walk up there tomorrow, if you like?"

"That would be fabulous, Robert."

We walked in silence for a while, arriving at the stone terraced cottage where I was staying. We went inside. We were alone. The living room smelt of soap and coal.

Sarah looked at me. I stared into her dazzling blue eyes.

She moved forward, stood on tiptoe, and kissed me. We stood like that, kissing for a while, and then I led her to the stairs, up to the bedroom, and we kissed again, my hands on her shoulders, her hands moving to rest on my hips.

She undressed me, and I undressed her. My hands slid down her rib cage, rested on her hips. She groaned, and pushed herself towards me. And then it happened so fast, it was a blur, surreal, and we were on the bed, kissing and touching, making love, and I was deep inside her, the whole experience a whirling moment in time where I forgot about the war, forgot about my childhood, and joined with this wonderful woman with the dazzling eyes, and gave her everything, gave her my love, and gave her my soul.

PART THREE

A PAGAN PLACE

WOODLAND DREAMS.
"THROUGH SHARPWOOD."
2ND. NOVEMBER 1903.

IN THE DISTANCE thunder rumbled, as if the gods were angry, arguing, complaining. The boy stepped out over the insane tangle of deadwood, and paused, one shoe slipping, to look down, *down* into the trench beneath him. Lightning flickered, illuminating the scene.

The branches appeared as bones.

Sharpened bones, ready to impale him . . .

With dry mouth he continued, stepping from branch to branch, arms outstretched for balance, licking his lips occasionally and glad of the cool rain on his face. The trench—that wound in the earth—was wider than it had first appeared. And with trembling limbs the boy crossed the treacherous place.

Water rolled from his face in rivulets, making his skin grey in the gloom. He coughed a harsh, chesty cough. And continued . . .

The deadwood shifted beneath him, suddenly, and he glanced down through the mad tangle, matted with leaves and mud and twigs. Several branches cracked hollow, deep in the depths, a terrible, frightening warning. The deadwood felt incredibly unstable, shifting like a creature beneath him, like a live thing. And bizarrely he moved as if he were riding a creature of wood, its cumbersome legs powerful as it churned through mud and leaves, and he was astride the beast, could feel the heavy thump of its heart beneath him, could see steam snorted from its great bark nostrils . . .

He blinked, coughed again, and shook his head with a shower of droplets. Thunder rumbled again; the boy crested a slight rise in the insanity tangle of deadwood, and began his descent, heart pounding in his ears, the smell of woodland sour and ripe in his nostrils, invading his every sense.

He glanced over his shoulder. And amidst the thickly gathered conifers, interspersed with beech and oak and ash, he could see *creatures* moving within the depths. There were *hundreds* of them, their grey eyes peering from the dense green darkness, their snouts hissing and snorting at this intrusion into their world, their land, their place of worship. Suddenly, the boy felt like an intruder, violator, a reaper of the woodland—and he was most definitely *not welcome.*

Their eyes gleamed, and he watched them dancing through the trees, heading towards him.

"No!" he cried, and slipped on wet wood, and a hefty

crack echoed through the silence. He felt himself sliding, falling, his hands searching for grip, flailing, shifting, the deadwood bucking and shifting its weight beneath him and his fist curled around a branch—and he prayed—and it held, and he steadied himself against the sharp, prodding spears of old white wood and closed his eyes for a moment in silent thanks. He had not fallen. Not fallen deep into the trench of splintered teeth which he now realised with absolute certainty would chew him up.

The boy nodded and, without looking back, scampered across the rest of the deadwood, even now fearing the return journey, so precarious was this most effective of barriers.

His shoes touched earth, moss and grass and broken twigs, and he stood panting on the woodland floor, shoes scratched and scuffed, knowing he would be in trouble with Mother when he got home, yet strangely not caring.

He was close. Closer than he had ever been!

Here, the woodland was huge, towering conifers. They swayed high above and he squinted, watching their mighty boughs shift, and creak, and squeak, and whisper. Whisper like ghosts.

The boy set off through the evergreens, breathing their heady perfume, Sharpwood left thankfully behind. A place of teeth, he realised. Glancing back, his eyes came to the trench and he saw the grey-eyed creatures there. They had stopped at the barrier, their muzzles sniffing his scent. They were similar to dogs but without any fur, their entire bodies carrying saggy, grey skin. Their eyes searched for him. Saliva strung from fangs. Their claws were black and long. Then the pack split in two, heading off in separate directions . . .

The boy shivered.

They were hunting him, whatever they were . . .

He drove on through the evergreens, pushing himself forward, sweat on his brow now as panic increased in his breast and he slipped, slid, pushed onwards. He burst into a clearing, and something fell through him—a feeling, cool and luxurious.

What is this new place?

This new . . . sanctuary?

It felt calm, and clean. It oozed purity, and the boy felt suddenly safe. As if the trees themselves would protect him from the creatures sniffing after his scent.

What to call it? What to call this new place . . .

"Soulwood," he whispered.

Something scampered to one side and the boy jumped, then ignored the sound when he realised it was something small; stooped, sometimes crawling, he progressed way through the conifers ahead, tightly packed now, and up a steep incline which presented itself.

The trees grew low, and the boy had to almost crouch,

head bowed low, branches and fern brushing his hair and clothes, touching him with a woodland intimacy. It was damp and musty down there with the roots and decaying leaves and pine needles, and the boy scraped his knees on limestone rocks protruding from the ground like teeth. The hill grew incredibly steep, and the boy could think of only two words as he crawled and panted and heaved up the slope. Two words that flooded his mind.

Hunter's Hill.

The moon was gone. She'd fled to a happier place.

The boy crawled in darkness, the powerful aroma of pine filling his mind with corrupt perfume as he used roots and rock to heave himself up the slope. His muscles were straining now, strength failing as he heaved and hauled himself onwards.

Yet he knew. Knew he was close, knew he was so, so close!

Behind, he heard a panting sound. A scrabbling. Not one set of claws, but many. He squinted for a few moments, terror taking his heart in its fist. Then he turned back and pushed himself on towards the summit.

In the surrounding darkness, a different type of beast watched. They had wooden eyes, their indecipherable faces lined with the bark of silver birch and staring unblinkingly through the black.

Lightning flickered in the far distance, an echo of

light through the heavy canopy.

The boy whimpered as he crawled.

Fear had taken hold of him.

He could smell these new beasts, with their damp-wood stink. Motionless, statues, watching, watching, watching . . .

Hunter's Hill!

Just up ahead!

And as he crawled, and struggled, up this final climb towards Heartwood, towards the Dream . . . all he could hear were his mother's words in his mind, muttering phrases from the Bible, words like wrath, fire and brimstone . . .

YPRES SALIENT (3RD. BATTLE OF).
"TOWARDS BOULOGNE."
13TH. JULY 1917.

GEORGE WEBB KISSED his sister on the cheek, trying hard to ignore her tears, which glistened like silver, but eventually letting his own fall free as he moved towards the wide walkway and the thick crowd of men trudging slowly across the brine-drenched wood.

"Goodbye, Marie."

"I'll miss you, George."

"And me, you."

He waved and smiled, summoning some kind of enthusiasm.

Marie waved back, kissing her fingers and then waving again. They had become very close since their mother's death only a month earlier. And now he was leaving her. Alone.

George turned, was swallowed by the sheer vast scale of the *Valiant* which rocked at her moorings. He was directed down narrow corridors and past scores of men laughing and joking, swapping tales of childhood and making new acquaintances. He found a place to camp down, surrounded by men performing similar actions, unrolled his bedroll, and made some space for himself. Life aboard the ship was going to be cramped, and Webb was filled with a silent dread at the thought of the front lines in France and Belgium.

George Webb was not a soldier, nor a warrior; he was a man in love with peace and life.

"I cannot do this," he'd whispered the night before, as they ate at the kitchen table, lit by golden candlelight.

"But you must," said Marie, smiling, beautiful eyes glowing with candle flame.

"I cannot use a rifle or a bayonet in battle—it's abhorrent! How can I stab steel into another man's body? To remove another person's life? It is wrong. It is evil."

"You've been drafted, my love. To protect us from the Hun. You must go." She held his hand then, eyes fierce. "You must do right by King and Country."

Webb had been drafted, along with thousands of other men—men from all counties across Britain, replacements for the forty-odd thousand Allied lives that had been lost on the Western Front in June of 1917.

Webb tugged at his rough canvas clothes, which smelled musty. He grunted, pulling his kitbag from beneath him, then leant his back against the hard metal wall of the ship and looked around. He was seated in what had once been a mess hall for sailors but was now confined quarters for thousands of anxious young men.

Webb shook his head.

"George!"

He looked up, and grinned suddenly at Robert Jones, who strode across the chamber, stepping over countless drafted Tommies all around. Jones reached his friend and they shook hands, and embraced.

"I've been looking for you for ages," smiled Jones, squeezing down beside Webb. Deep below in the bowels of the *Valiant,* the oil-fired engines rumbled into life, sending throbbing vibrations through the walls. The floor shuddered.

"I feel sick," said Webb.

"But we haven't bloody set sail yet!" said Jones, smiling, patting Webb's arm. In a more serious voice, he added, "Don't worry, mate; when we're out at sea and you've thrown up a few times, you'll get used to it. I did."

"Thanks. It'll be something to look forward to."

Jones nodded, and looked around at the grumbling men. He could feel their apprehension, could appreciate their panic at the thought of fighting on the front. Some of these lads had received . . . what? Two weeks training? At least Jones had put in serious time on the front lines, had fought on the Somme at Flers-Courcelette and Transloy Ridges. At least he had lived through his experiences, learned from his time in the mud, learned of pain through bullets and shrapnel and seeing his friends massacred.

And now you're going back, whispered a devilish voice in his mind. Jones half-wished he hadn't made a full recovery from the shrapnel in his body. Half-wished he was still unfit for service, that the last eight months which had seen so many, many fatalities on both sides of the front had not seen fit to give him full mobility. He half-wished he had lost a leg, or an arm . . .

Jones shook his head. *Shit, no,* he decided. He had seen many men without limbs in the hospitals, on the recovery wards back on Blighty soil. Chaps without limbs had curiously dulled eyes. But then, what was more important? An arm, or your life?

Yet, being whole, being repaired, had condemned him once more to battle.

And that was just the way it was.

Jones settled back, chatting to Webb, whom he'd known since childhood. Jones was six years Webb's senior, but their mothers had been good friends and this had been good reason for the two lads to form a friendship which had endured over the years, despite Jones's spate of heavy drinking and gambling.

Now Webb had at last been drafted, concurrent with Jones's return to active service and mere coincidence—or fate—putting them aboard the same ship on the same day. Jones had seen Webb only once in the last month since the younger lad's mother had died, and Webb was pale, skin drawn tight, eyes lowered. He looked as if he'd lost weight, and Jones appraised his old friend with sadness. He gave a little shake of his head.

Webb caught the movement and turned his eyes on Jones. "What? What's the matter?"

"It's you, George. Look at you! You've not been feeding yourself properly."

"You know how it is," said Webb, his voice soft. "Since my mother ... well, you know how it is. Marie is a good cook, but it's not the same. Our house is no longer the same. It's lost some of its ... energy."

"She would have been proud of you now, though," said Jones, trying to lighten the mood. "She would have seen you in that uniform and been right proud!"

"No, she wouldn't, Rob. Stop trying to gee me up; it's no bloody use. Listen. I know you talked to her before she died. What did she say?"

"She knew you were going to be drafted," said Jones.

Webb snorted. "That wouldn't have taken a genius. The bastards have been working their way through the entire population of Great Britain! It had to come sooner or later. I just wish it had been later. I don't know if I can do this, Jones."

"She wanted me to look after you, George. She

wanted to see you taken care of. She made me promise."

Webb smiled, eyes full of tears. "She was a soft bugger, really, wasn't she?"

"Aye. Yes. A soft bugger."

The two men sat in comfortable silence for a while, and Jones remembered Webb's mother, a gentle woman, with soft features and luxurious curled brown hair. Her face had been deeply sunken when last they met, and the expression on her face told him all. She knew she was dying. Knew she was nearing the end of her mortal coil. She made Jones promise to look after her boy, her Little Georgie ... and Jones had promised because, ——, there had been no other option; because he owed her that much, a tiny morsel of comfort in her last days of pain.

She smiled through her haze of morphine. "Thank you, Robert Jones," she'd said. "I bless you under the watchful eye of God."

———

They docked at Boulogne and were transported by truck and on foot to camps behind the front lines. Jones bribed a corporal to alter Webb's posting, and when Bainbridge roared up on a BSA motorcycle, the two men watched the recently promoted sergeant stride through the darkness.

In the distance, the roar of an air offensive against the German Fourth Army was in progress, and the dulled sounds of machine guns drifted through the chatter of soldiers' talk and the grinding of bombs.

"Jones!" bellowed Bainbridge, throwing his arms around his friend and lifting the smaller man completely from his feet. Bainbridge was a little bit wilder and a little bit more tufted but the same man he'd befriended so long ago in a Cockney drinking pit. "It's damned good to see you!" he roared, voice louder than any Fritz machine gun.

Jones was laughing, and thumped Bainbridge in the chest as the Tommy lowered him to the ground. "God, man, you look old!" he said as he stared into the soldier's face. "And by God, you're a bloody sergeant now!" He flicked an imaginary speck of dust from the stripes embroidered on Bainbridge's arm. "I never would have thought it, letting such bad ——ing elements into the privileged ranks."

"Shut it, Jones!" boomed Bainbridge, through several new broken teeth. "But good, eh, lad? I've been practising, like, and I've the right temperament for my rank, now—or so Captain Myers tells me, the stinking old goat. Who's your friend?"

"This is Private George Webb, a childhood friend,"

said Jones, and Webb and Bainbridge shook hands, Bainbridge crushing his fingers. "Now, you look after him, Bainbridge. No ordering him to slop out the latrine trench!"

"Somebody's got to do it," grumbled Bainbridge. "But I like him! He has a strong grip; we'll see if that grip can be put to good use against Fritzy, eh, lad?" Bainbridge boomed out raucous laughter, but Webb merely smiled, a modest gesture that went unnoticed by Bainbridge as his colossal appetite for humour and madness took hold.

"So, then, tell me, how's life back in England?" asked Bainbridge, as Jones led his two friends into the camp behind the Yser Canal, and towards the canvas shelter which was home to more than thirty men.

They ducked and entered the shelter. "Oh, you know," said Jones, "the smell of home-cooking on a Sunday, roast chicken, roast potatoes, sprouts, juicy gravy, filling the warm house with that gorgeous aroma and making your mouth water . . ."

"Really?" said Bainbridge, licking his lips.

"Not really," conceded Jones. "Rations are tight and there's a roaring black market for anybody with the money. But Blighty is better than here; it's better than the mud and guns. At least you can get whisky and have the odd bet. At least there are women."

"Aye," said Bainbridge, nodding. "I wish I'd stayed

home longer, but with the call of the war, and all that . . . you know how it is. You should have seen it last week, though; do you remember Matchstick? No, he came after you left, I think. The bastards poured gas grenades into our trench . . . It was a close thing. I've been practising getting my mask on and off—seemed kind of important at the time, although a lot of the lads were moaning like whores in a German brothel. Well, Matchstick and some of the others couldn't get their masks on and we tried to help them, Christ we tried, but during the attack, the poor bastards choked to death."

Jones ran a hand through his recently shaved hair, aware this talk was making Webb uncomfortable. Webb took out a brush and polish and began cleaning his boots. Jones changed the subject.

"Bainbridge, remember that Beholla you smuggled back to Blighty?"

Bainbridge grinned, then looked carefully around. When he was sure nobody was looking, he slid it from beneath his coat and handed it to Jones. "Still have it, mate. Be careful; it's loaded."

"Loaded? Where did you get the ammo?"

"Scavenging, lad, scavenging. For souvos. But with this, it's worth it. That pistol has saved my life on many occasions! You should see their faces when you shoot them—ha ha! The bullets are designed so if you shoot a man in the forehead, it leaves nothing but a small hole but blows the back of his head off! I tell you, surprise isn't in it, mate."

Jones handed back the weapon with a small shiver, and Bainbridge hid it in his coat. He gave a theatrical wink, then gestured to Webb. "Your pal. He's a bit on the quiet side, like."

"Missing home," explained Jones.

Bainbridge slapped Webb on the back, and the Tommy coughed. "Missing your woman, eh, lad? I bet you've a nice lass waiting for you back home."

"No," said Webb, shaking his head.

There was a nearby explosion, and the ground shook. Jones's equipment rattled in his kitbag.

"Damn, those boys are getting too close!" snarled Bainbridge, surging to his feet and running out into the night. Overhead in the darkness, a plane droned into the black. "We're on your side, you fools!" screamed Bainbridge, hawking and spitting in the churned mud.

He turned to where Jones had followed him out. There was no sign of Webb.

"That young friend of yours is a strange bugger," said Bainbridge, eyes narrowing. "Out here, fear will get you killed readily as any ——ing bullet. And he's scared as a virgin on his wedding night."

Jones nodded, and followed Bainbridge towards his

motorcycle, where the sergeant lit two cigarettes, handing one to Jones.

Jones inhaled, and coughed harshly. "What the —— is that?"

"Bloody French tobacco," smiled Bainbridge. "Rough as a priest's cassock, and probably tastes the same. Not that I've had the privilege." He winked.

Jones scratched at his forehead, then said, "Look, Bainbridge, don't keep digging at Webb, will you? I know you're a bastard for it, because last year, you wouldn't leave me alone about the whisky and the gambling. Just go easy on him, all right? He hasn't done anything wrong."

Bainbridge dropped his cigarette and ground it into the mud under the heel of his boot. "If he's soft, then there's no place for him in my column."

Jones nodded.

"Anyway. Horse shit. It's nice to see you again, Rob, damned nice." Bainbridge patted Jones's cheek. "I'll arrange it so you can share my dugout in the trench. The guy who's with me now snores like a ——ing steam engine. Or a humping pig. Maybe both. He can sleep in the mud tomorrow, the lousy ——er."

Bainbridge climbed aboard his motorcycle and, on the fourth attempt, kicked it into life. Over the rumble of the engine, Jones said, "Is there room there for Webb as well?"

"Tell me you're joking, Jones?"

"No joke. I . . . I kind of promised his mother I'd look after him."

Bainbridge's laughter was loud and booming, and with slitted headlamp barely lighting the way, he roared off into the night, leaving Jones standing with the foul-smelling French cigarette.

Jones dropped the stub and walked back to camp, and in the darkness, the cigarette smouldered for a while, a tiny glow against an infinity of black.

Slowly, the mud dragged the stub down, embraced it, smothered it, and the glow was permanently extinguished.

YPRES SALIENT (3RD. BATTLE OF).
18TH. JULY 1917.

SHORTLY AFTER DAWN, the artillery bombardment of the Ypres Ridge and the German Fourth began. The Germans had spent the previous year turning their front lines into well-fortified positions defended by hundreds of concrete pillboxes housing heavy machine guns.

The way for Allied advance had been paved by constant air attacks during the previous five days, the bombs turning No Man's Land and the surrounding countryside into a mire of devastation—a landscape of oblivion obscured by a haze of smoke, gas, and the breath of a dark god intent on massacre.

Now the boom, whine, and crash of mortar shells and field guns echoed across the land with the intention of pounding German defensive lines into pulp, thus allowing infantry from the British Fifth and French First an easier push towards St. Julien and Passchendaele.

Only time would tell if the strategy would work . . .

YPRES SALIENT (3RD. BATTLE OF).
"THE TRENCHES."
22ND. JULY 1917.

BAINBRIDGE WASN'T CONVINCED. "Gough has his head up his ——ing backside," he complained as Jones helped him shovel scattered earth from the floor of the dugout into iron buckets.

"How so?" grunted Jones, heaving a shovel of earth into the container and wiping the sweat from his brow with a yellowed handkerchief.

"The weather," said Bainbridge, simply. "They've been pounding the enemy lines to —— for the last four days, and there's no sign of them slowing. Add that on top of the savage, non-stop air bombardments, and we've got a recipe for disaster. All it takes is a little rain, and *we're* the poor bastards who'll have to slog out there up to our tits in mud."

"Yeah. Well. I suppose the brass hats know what they're doing," said Jones, and watched Bainbridge heave the bucket up the steps from the dugout. When he returned, he threw the bucket into a corner, where it clattered to a halt on its side.

Jones had settled down into trench life once more, happy at least he wasn't going over the bags for several days. Webb, on the other hand, was a constant bundle of nerves, although he tried not to let it show. Unfortunately, Bainbridge was an expert at spotting a man's fear from a hundred paces, and their crossing paths had been nothing but painful for Webb.

Jones tried to explain it to his old friend the previous night, whilst Bainbridge was out directing a group of Tommies in the digging out of a collapsed communications trench.

"It's just his way, George."

Webb shrugged. "I don't ——ing like the man. He looks at me with a sneer on his face, just because he's seen action, just because he's proven himself in battle! Well, I don't know how I'll perform; maybe I will crack up, maybe I will 'run away from the bullets' like your good friend suggested. But he has no right to deride me until I'm proven or disproven."

"I think it's because you were drafted in," Jones said, at last. "I've seen Bainbridge snarling at other new conscripts. He sees the fact that you had to be dragged in by your lapels instead of volunteering like us earlier men, a kind of betrayal."

"Yes, well, that's his view. We all carry ghosts, Robert, and I just wish Bainbridge would let mine lie. I wish he would leave me alone. Remember what you said when I visited you in that London hospital? You could hardly move your arms or legs because of the shrapnel, and you looked into my eyes, swore, cursed the trenches, and told me never to join up; *you* told me never, ever to join up. Do you remember that, Rob?"

"I remember. And I didn't want to come back now. But for some men—and Bainbridge is one of them—war becomes a way of life. To Bainbridge, other men are soldiers willing to throw themselves into the breach, or cowards ready to run home to Mummy. That's how his mind works; you're either with him or against him. There is no in-between. No shades of grey."

Webb trudged off into the night, face a scowl, and Jones swore to himself he'd talk with the sergeant. Do what he could to help Webb. But when he approached Bainbridge, the big man laughed it off with the words "We'll see when we go over the top, eh, laddie? We'll see if he's ——ing king or coward."

———

Webb knelt on the mud-smeared plank, hammer in hand as he repaired the lengths of broken duckboard. He and seven other men had been detailed to the far end of the trench where an 18-pounder British field gun had become unknowingly blocked, forcing a misfire, wounding six men, putting the gun out of action, and causing damage to the trench walls and the duckboards.

Taking another plank of wood, he put it in place, held a thick nail steady, and began to hammer it through the timber. His mind began to wander, seeking to block out the noise of the booming guns. A nearby explosion of return fire showered the trench with dirt and Webb ducked, a movement that had become second nature since arriving in the trenches, and he continued to hammer, thinking back to Wales, and home, and the long days by his mother's bedside . . .

George, you look well today!

How was your day at work, my boy? I've been reading . . . Would you like to listen? Yes, sit there . . . just put it on that stool. There shall come forth a shoot from the stump of Jesse, and a branch shall grow out of his roots. And the spirit of the LORD shall rest upon him, the spirit of wisdom and understanding, the spirit of counsel and might, the spirit of knowledge and fear of the LORD. And his delight shall be in the fear of the LORD . . . in the fear . . .

Your sister has made some dinner. It's in the oven. She's dating that Broome lad from down the street; you know the one, with bushy black hair. They're going to a dance tonight . . . She looked beautiful in her blue dress; it matched her eyes, made her look so incredibly beautiful!

George, pass me ... pass me my glass of water, please. I have to take ... my tablets. The doctor will be annoyed if I don't take my tablets.

Good evening, George. Thanks, my dear. Where have you been today? Oh, yes, that's right, that's interesting, dear.

Your father would have been so proud of you! Have you heard ... have you heard how it goes on the front?

Take my ration book; go and get yourself some eggs. You look starved, you poor lad. Oh, yes, you do; now, go on, before your old mam puts her foot behind your backside and kicks you down those stairs ...

I'm sorry ... sorry, George. I don't feel quite myself today. Oh, don't go on so; I don't look anything of the sort. Please can you ... oh, God ... can you pass me my tablets? There's a dear ...

Does it hurt? Yes, George, it hurts. I feel like I've been cursed, although I don't know what ... what for ...

—a gentle, pain-filled smile, spreading slowly across her face—

Maybe that is part of my curse, son, that fact that I don't know from whence my enemy strikes ...

Pass me my Bible; there's a good lad ...

When you offer a sacrifice of peace offerings to the LORD, you shall offer it so that you may be accepted ...

—flicking through pages and reading at random—

Hark, a tumult on the mountains as of a great multitude!

Hark, an uproar of kingdoms, of nations gathering together! The LORD of hosts is mustering a host for battle. They come from a distant land, from the end of the heavens, the LORD and the weapons of his indignation, to destroy the whole earth . . .

He could see her in the gloom. She was sleeping, and he did not wake her, did not want to see her in pain—and so he pulled over a stool and sat beside her bed, his eyes tracing the weary lines of her face, the sunken hollows where once there had been flesh, the dark rings where once there had been joy.

"How could this happen to you?" he whispered, but expected no answers. At first, he had blamed the doctors for not being able to cure her; then he blamed the world, for apparently cursing her; and finally, he had blamed God for failing to step in and heal her.

Now . . . he blamed nobody. He simply sat in silent misery, watching his mother, watching Mary Webb, watching this fine woman he had known for seventeen years, who had raised him lovingly from cradle . . . nurtured him through childhood, watching her gradually erode and die.

All he would be able to do is bury her in a poor man's grave.

———————

"She has a lump in her stomach, George. She has a cancer, spreading through her digestive tract, eating at her flesh as well as her will to live."

"A lump?"

"A tumour, in her stomach. It is too large for us to operate; it must have been causing her incredible pain."

"Yes . . . yes, she has had pain for a while."

"Did she not seek medical advice? Did she visit the doctor?"

"She did . . . or she told us she did. A tumour, you say? I'm confused . . . will she die? Will she die?"

Echoing softly in his mind.

"Will she die?"

"Yes, George. She will die. I'm sorry."

———————

Jones walked through the dark trench, like a carved wound in the earth, carrying a tray with care as he skipped over puddles, trying not to splash his trousers. He reached the steps of the dugout and heard laughter within, but not the laughter of humour, more the laughter of bitterness, of mockery . . .

He stood there, shivering slightly, the gypo on the tray steaming and smelling almost good enough to eat. In the distance, the heavy artillery bombardment of the enemy lines continued into the night; it was a song of metal, a symphony of pain and death.

"You're always writing bloody letters, soldier. Who are you writing to now, eh?" came Bainbridge's voice. Jones frowned and moved forward but stopped at the next exchange of words.

"Shut up, Bainbridge."

"To you, it's *sergeant*, and don't forget it or I'll break that pretty face of yours. So, come on, who are you writing to? A slut back home ... or maybe your mother? Yes, a boy like you wouldn't know a real woman if she lay down before you with legs spread wide open. So then, it's to Mummy, eh? Mummy's little boy ..."

"Shut up!"

"What you writing? Asking her to pull some strings, get you drafted back to Blighty, eh, lad? Away from the fighting? Away from the death? Get yourself posted to some nice little base in England, guarding against the never never never ... while over here in France, your comrades are getting shelled to ——ing pieces!"

"That's not true. Leave me alone, Bainbridge, leave me alone ..."

"Can't you take the truth, little Mummy's boy? Can't

you take it? Well, remember this: I'm the sergeant here, and somebody has to read the letters sent home, somebody..."

"You read them?"

"They've got to be read. National security, lad; we can't have you leaking secrets to the ——ing Hun and having Mr Crumps for breakfast as a result of your flapping big mouth."

"Enough!" hissed Jones, stooping low to enter the dugout. "Bainbridge, leave the lad alone, will you? The poor bastard has been through enough!"

Bainbridge laughed. "Been through enough, has he? He's a spineless bugger, and he deserves bloody shooting! Always writing letters home ... you little Mummy's boy! You hear me, Webb? And as for you, Jones ... we were shrapp'd together, man; we're brothers! Don't side with the new recruits; they ain't worth it."

Bainbridge pushed his way from the dugout and left behind an atmosphere of tense oppression. Jones moved to his bunk and sat down, stared over at where Webb was poised, his pen touching the paper but not actually moving.

"Are you all right?"

"Why does he hate me, Rob?"

"He doesn't hate you."

"You heard him ... He thinks I deserve shooting!

And he kept calling me a Mummy's boy . . . That hurts me inside; it twists me . . ."

"He doesn't know, George. He doesn't know about your mother. Maybe if I told him what you'd been through?"

Webb looked up, his tear-filled eyes suddenly angry. "What? And endure his ——ing sympathy?" he spat. "You never sat there holding her ——ing clawed, clenching hand whilst she cried like a babe; you never sat there while she screamed and moaned and begged me to kill her. And I thought about it. I looked at that pillow and thought about smothering her . . . to put her out of her pain. When she finally died, I was glad, you hear me? I was glad because it was an end to suffering, an end to the constant agony. In the end, even the drugs didn't take away the pain. If I'd had a gun, I swear I would have shot her myself."

"You don't mean that, George," said Jones.

"I mean it, Rob. And I tell you something else; when I finally do go over the top, then your friend Sergeant Bainbridge is going to get one hell of a shock, because every bastard I shoot down will be for my mother, because I want them to suffer like she suffered, I want God to hear the screams of the people I send his way, and I'm going to laugh and spit in his ugly ——ing face when I see him. And if I don't see God? Well, then, I'll be in hell, exactly where I deserve." Webb threw down his pen and, grabbing his coat, left the dugout.

Jones saw tears streaming down the soldier's face but let him go. He had no words, no answers for the young man, and for several minutes, he considered going after Bainbridge and beating the living shit out of the man for his thoughtlessness, stupidity, and lack of humanity.

Finally, Jones lay back on his bunk and calmed his breathing. The candlelight played across the far wall, and Jones watched the shadows, trying to clear his mind, trying to calm himself.

He thought about Sarah. Back in Wales. He remembered meeting up with her. Kissing her. Holding her. Dancing with her. Laughing together ... making love together under rough blankets as the rain drummed against the window ...

Drinking whisky with her.

Her eyes, flashing with hate, tears on her cheeks, as she threw a glass at him ... the sound as it shattered against the wall.

The sound of breaking glass, and Sarah, sobbing ...

Shadows flickered lazily, dancing this way and that, swaying like trees. Like towering conifers ... swaying in the night storm.

Jones closed his eyes and allowed sleep to take him, for he was bone weary and sick to death of the trenches.

And he dreamed of the woods, climbing the steep slope on muddy hands and knees as, behind, creatures snarled in the darkness.

WOODLAND DREAMS.
"TOWARDS HEARTWOOD."
2ND. NOVEMBER 1903.

HARK, A TUMULT on the mountains as of a great multitude!
Hark, an uproar of kingdoms, of nations gathering together!

The boy struggled on, clawing the ground, rain dripping from the vast overhead canopy. It ran down his face and he rubbed at his eyes, coughing harshly, and he began to shiver and he coughed again, alarmed when mucus spurted between his fingers. A coldness crept into his bones and he wished, wished to God that his feet were dry and warm, and what he would give to be in a warm bed with hot soup inside him and to be happy and safe and warm . . .

He could hear the snarling creatures, coming up the hill behind him. Their claws gouged the earth. They panted, muzzles dripping strings of saliva, their grey eyes fixed on him, struggling onwards . . .

Nearly there . . .

Hunter's Hill . . .

Heartwood . . .

With a cry, he reached the summit of the slope, his hand grasping a hefty branch as the creature was nearly upon him. He spun around on his backside, and as the first creature leapt, he swung the branch, which struck it between the eyes, knocking it to one side, whining and snapping fangs.

There were three of them, and the boy scrambled to his feet and backed out into the woodland clearing. Thunder rumbled. Lightning crackled, lighting the scene with bright blue electric.

"Come on!" screamed the boy as the three creatures advanced. He heard more snarls from further down the hill. Lips curled back over long silver fangs, and with a blink, the boy realised the lips were like ebony, the teeth like sharpened wooden splinters, the fur like grey moss, the eyes like pale knots in pine.

They're like dogs, he thought. *Dogs created by the woodland itself . . .*

Another leapt, and the branch connected with its skull, whacking it to the side where it yelped; the boy took the branch in both hands now, and a bright beaming confidence overtook him.

"Come on. I'll kill you all," he screamed, his young voice ringing out across the clearing.

The three creatures observed him, panting, and he began to back away. They stood, chests heaving, drenched by the rain. Their pale eyes followed him, but they no longer attacked.

He backed away, away, and watched as more of the dog-like creatures appeared at the edge of the trees. Their eyes watched him. Fear filled his chest as he realised, now, there were more than he'd first thought . . .

Ten. Fifteen. Twenty.

His eyes were wide, but he kept a firm hold on the branch as his shoes trod backwards.

Again, the land sloped upwards through the clearing. He glanced over his shoulder and could see it!

The summit of Hunter's Hill, shrouded in mist, containing huge shapes, their dim outlines filling him with a sudden faith.

Hunter's Hill. He could feel the mystery, the essence of legend, the weight of the myths beneath his scuffed shoes, beneath his feet, beneath the limestone rock and thin soil and carpet of sodden, rotting leaves and wood.

Hunter's Hill.

The Gateway to Heartwood.

"I must go on," he said, shaking his branch at the creatures who watched him from the darkness. "Towards the Heartwood!"

He broke into a run, shoes pounding and slipping

on the long grass. Wind whipped through his hair. Rain trickled down his face, down his neck. Thunder rumbled, ominous and growling.

He glanced behind, but the dog-creatures did not follow, instead staying by the edge of the trees, as if they were connected to that segment of woodland, unable to leave the trees to which they were joined . . .

The boy slowed as he neared the objects on the summit of Hunter's Hill. They were larger than he'd seen in his dreams, seven of them in a circle, towering up above the soil and stranded twigs and branches. Each was five times the height of a man and carved from the lightning-blasted core of an ancient oak. They had been carved—with skill, each to resemble a different figure—limbs twisted and bent, faces curled into grotesque gargoyle growls.

The boy drew near, and slowed, and stopped. The branch he carried slipped from his fingers as he came to the edge of the circle, and moved forward, to stand at the very centre of Hunter's Hill, turning slowly, looking up at these huge carved figures.

He stared at the carvings from a long-dead race. And they gazed *inwards*, not outwards, on the summit of Hunter's Hill. Their twisted limbs and massive bulks glistening under their rain and mist cloaks. They were beautiful. They were ancient. They were perfect.

The boy gasped . . .

Each figure was a man. Some wore masks, with huge circular eyes. In their hands they carried rifles and swords. Many had two mouths, their faces lifted to the sky in double silent screams . . .

"Wow," he whispered.

Then, "I am here. As I promised. As you commanded."

The boy coughed again, a heavy cough, and pain was in him now, deep in his chest, and he was coughing, coughing, coughing and the mucus was dribbling down his chin and he could not stop the coughing, and he felt weak, as weak as a lamb, and he tried to lift his eyes to see the images more clearly, these wooden totems of long-dead days, but he no longer had the strength . . . and the rain ran down his body, and he sank to the ground, laid himself on the cold earth at the centre of the circle, and he curled into a ball and coughed up mucus and lay there thinking about what he had witnessed, what he could feel coursing through the ground under his fingers, beneath his body, the energy of a different place, a different time, a different world.

His eyes fixed on the huge carved figures, one by one by one.

They seemed to speak to him, with cold dead mouths.

You will come to us, they said.

One day, you will fight with us.

One day, you will save us.

And everything drifted in smoke, and the ground was cold, and his coughing would not stop, and he lay there, and he waited to die.

He could hear his mother's words echoing in his mind, could still see that religious glint in her eyes as fresh as tears. And her words, her words harsh, forcing down the corridors of his soul . . .

Hark, a tumult on the mountains as of a great multitude!

Hark, an uproar of kingdoms, of nations gathering together!

The LORD of hosts is mustering a host for battle.

They come from a distant land, from the end of the heavens, the LORD and the weapons of his indignation, to destroy the whole earth.

———————

Hands curled around him. Lifted his unconscious body into the air. And the Skogsgrå drew him to her chest as her eyes met the eyes of the Huldra, who gave a single nod, and they set off through trees as old as the world.

———————

They found him the next morning at the foot of the sprawling bracken leading from Clearwood. When the boy hadn't returned, and his mother found his bed empty, she panicked. The boy's father was down in London on business, and so his mother, alone and frightened, ran to a neighbour's house to raise the alarm.

————

As dawn brightened the sky with streaks of violet, a search party set out from the boy's house under cold grey drizzle.

He was almost dead. Damp, cold, and unresponsive. They wrapped him in blankets and carried him back to his house. The doctor was sent for, arriving by carriage twenty minutes later, his breath reeking of whisky.

The boy was diagnosed with pulmonary tuberculosis, early stages, and as such could be treated at the local sanatorium. The doctor hurriedly prepared admittance papers for the boy's incarceration, and amidst his mother's tears, he was transported by ambulance to the distant Victorian building to begin treatment. The boy's mother did not travel with him.

————

Robert Jones awoke just once in the ambulance, looking around, eyes wide, coughing and choking, eyes streaming tears; in his head he could hear a booming, crashing sound, as of endless trees collapsing deep within ancient woodland.

A nurse held his hand, patted his arm, smiled down at him with absolute kindness.

"The evil thing, it's hiding, in the Heartwood," Jones whispered, and closed his eyes, and slept a dreamless sleep filled with pain and anguish and a need to return to the trees which seemed to stretch out for ever, and ever, and ever.

PART FOUR

A SILENT SONG

YPRES SALIENT (3RD. BATTLE OF).
"OVER THE WIRE."
1ST. AUGUST 1917.

JONES HAD A DREAM that night. A nightmare played out under blackened trees. He was in the trench like a curved scar created by a razor. He looked left and right, across the muddied, stained duckboards.

He was alone, and the fear started to eat him.

Whistles sounded, and Jones gripped his rifle tight, clambered up the ladder, over the wire, out into No Man's Land and the enveloping darkness of the bomb-blasted forest. Burnt trees surrounded him, twisted and angular.

They ate him whole.

Turning to look back, Jones could no longer see the trench.

Guns roared in the distance beyond the scorched woodland, and mortar shells exploded, kicking up great mushrooms of mud and earth and roots, shattering the broken woodland trees around him.

Jones stood, gazing at the trees which had once been so majestic, so holy, and now were nothing more than broken, bent, smashed figures returning charred to the earth which had spawned them.

Out there in the gloom of No Man's Land, Jones could distinguish shapes, giant silhouettes looming as if carved from the night... They were tanks, belching fumes, tracks grinding through mud and crushing bent trees... but even as he watched, the roaring of their engines faded and they ground to a halt, rocking, and stood in silence, obsolete amidst the crushed woodland.

A bullet sped past Jones's ear, catching the lapel of his coat, but he did not flinch. The guns had stopped.

They could not kill him now.

He walked forward, boots sinking in the mud, until he reached the first tank. It was a Mark IV, its six-pounders silent and still, its great riveted tracks motionless in the mud, and mangled with the broken branches of dead trees, like splinters caught in a beast's maw.

Jones walked slowly along the side of the machine, running a hand down the dirt-smeared planks of riveted steel, until he was past the monstrosity and walking through the skeletal woods.

He turned once. The Tank Mark IV was motionless. But to Jones's eyes, in this place of hell, the tank seemed suddenly carved from wood, black, charred, scarred wood, as if the tank itself had grown from the shell-pounded earth.

He walked, picking his way through the remains of the trees, their branches reaching out to him, begging him. He saw a sprawled corpse nearby, and it was Bainbridge; for a moment it appeared the large Tommy had been carved from wood, from black deadwood, but as Jones moved closer, he gave a humourless laugh. He knelt and touched the Tommy, the corpse without eyes.

The body was hard, bark-covered, a fallen tree trunk which somehow resembled his friend.

He heard a sound. A whisper of cloth. And looked up.

They were there. Three of these . . . *walriders*. They loomed over Jones and stared down at him, muzzles drooling, glittering eyes fixed on him.

Jones stood, and lifted his rifle, licking his lips.

They grinned at him.

"We meet again, little man."

"You do not frighten me."

"We should. We hunt you through dreams and through reality. We want your eyes."

"Why would you want my eyes?"

"You have seen things we also want to see."

Jones lifted his rifle and fired, the bullet screaming on a discharge of ignition. It entered the middle walrider's eye, exiting from the back of its skull on a shower of bone. The creature rocked back but then dropped, claws gouging the earth. It snarled, and leapt at Jones, the other two also leaping forward, one to either side. Jones's rifle came up, and he leant back, wedging the stock of the rifle into the mud. The walrider literally impaled itself, charging onto his bayonet. Blood showered from its muzzle, spraying Jones, who squatted, transfixed, as this creature pushed itself slowly up his blade with squelching sounds, the wound widening, then further, up the muzzle of his rifle, the hole in its chest getting bigger, and bigger . . .

They stopped, locked. The other walriders halted, claws flexing in mud. The walrider on Jones's bayonet grinned at him, at his blood-spattered countenance, its muzzle scant inches from his face.

"You can taste me now."

Jones gritted his teeth, and said nothing.

"You have drank down my blood. We are part of one another."

"Horse shit."

"You think you have won, little soldier?" it snarled on fetid, poisonous breath worse than any Hun gas attack. "This is simply the beginning . . ."

"Jones!"

Jones shuddered, recoiling from the terrifying image, the horrifying experience, and then he was falling, and with a creak of branches, claws came up, jerking, and twig fingers reached for him, grasped at him . . .

———————

"Jones!"

He opened his eyes. Bainbridge was shaking his shoulder and he almost screamed, images flickering, but managed to clamp his mouth shut, grinding his teeth, banishing visions of a haunted No Man's Land from his skull.

"They hunt me," he whispered.

"What's that, lad?"

"Nothing," croaked Jones, sitting up and rubbing his eyes. "What's up, Sergeant?"

Bainbridge's smile was a flash of teeth in the gloom.

"Load your rifle, soldier. The command has come through to advance on the Hun and finish this thing once and for all."

———————

The men assembled in the trench under a downpour of rain. It had been raining all night, and the heavily bombarded ground of No Man's Land was a treacherous mire.

"Hit them hard!" Bainbridge was shouting, in his rousing speech to build morale, but Jones ignored his words, looked away from the anger and hate in the sergeant's face. Once, they had been friends. Once, they had been brothers. Now that was slipping away. Bainbridge had changed, and Jones was loath to admit that his friend had become a demon.

Where has his humanity gone?

His compassion?

Ha.

Pissed away in shell holes, that's where.

Whistles wept from amidst the driving rain. Men scrambled forward, up and over to glory beyond.

Webb was in front of Jones, his back straight, head held high, SMLE clasped in clammy hands as they sank ankle-deep in mud and headed towards the distant enemy lines, gloomy through the dark and the smoke.

Guns echoed. The men heaved through mud, a great line of infantry sweeping in from left and right under the cover of heavy machine gun fire; the considerable airborne and artillery bombardments of the last twenty days had destroyed much of the opposing lines, or so they'd been told, but there was still resistance, including chipped, battered concrete pillboxes housing terrible machines of death.

Bullets slapped through the mud to Jones's right, cutting down a line of men in a shower of screams and blood.

"Get down!" screamed Jones, and Webb hit the

ground in front as more bullets whined close by.

Bainbridge was far to Jones's right, organising a small attack force, bullets keeping the men pinned down. "You two, follow me!" he bellowed, and the group of men crawled through the mud until they were sheltered and hiding behind the ragged remains of a fallen, scorched tree. An oak, scarred beyond all recognition.

"This is madness," said Webb, eyes wide and staring at Jones.

Jones gave a nod. "Welcome to the front lines," he said, with a curious neutrality.

"You see that pillbox?" growled Bainbridge, mad eyes roving over the group of men. "We're taking it. Ready your weapons."

"We'll be cut down!" wailed Webb.

"——ing do it, or you'll be shot for disobeying an order."

Webb nodded.

Jones growled something incomprehensible.

Then they were up, ten of them, and storming up the sloping, churned ground. Jones's eyes narrowed. Muzzle flashes flickered from the pillbox slit and he aimed, firing off three shots at the dark eye.

More men joined the charge, emerging from the smoke, eyes wide, faces either scared or twisted into snarls.

Bullets ripped through mud before him, ricocheting from a large chipped rock to Jones's left. He tore his eyes from Bainbridge's heroic assault and glanced around for Webb, but the Tommy had vanished, blending into the charging line of infantry ahead.

"Webb?" he called, dragging himself to his feet, clothes heavy with mud, colours unrecognisable.

He ran on, through the rain.

———

Bainbridge ducked a volley of bullets and turned to the two men behind him, but they were no longer there. They were corpses twisted on the ground.

"Bastard."

He ran on, jumped down, crouched in a shell hole, watching the flashes from the Bergmann beyond the concrete slit. Bullets roared and Bainbridge waited patiently, counting, estimating. His ears picked up the series of clicks and he surged to his feet, pounding through the mud towards the pillbox as if his life depended on it. Which it did. Bainbridge knew a Bergmann machine gun had a curved ammunition box which could hold a two hundred–round belt. As he ran, he realised he had, what? Twenty seconds? Ten? Then they'd replace the belt and scythe him down . . .

A pistol cracked, a bullet whistling nearby. Bainbridge pumped a couple of rounds at the hole and saw chips of concrete erupt. And then he was past, crawling across dirt, the rear of the pillbox opening fast, a gun appearing. Bainbridge fired three shots from his Beholla, listened to the screams as the German went down, gurgling. Bainbridge could see a leg twitching.

But how many were there?

He moved carefully to the pillbox entrance, then glanced about. The door was slightly ajar, chipped by bullets. Leaning slowly to one side, he fired off a couple of shots into the split of black. There was a *whump* and slap. He heard a groan, and from inside came a thump, as of a body falling to the ground.

Silence.

Bainbridge kicked open the door, firing off his last shots into the darkness where they flickered sparks from the metal housing of the machine gun. Then he grinned.

"——ing brilliant!"

He crept inside, scanning the interior. The two Hun were dead.

"Got you, you bastards."

There came a crack, and a flash from the floor. In disbelief, in that split second, Bainbridge saw the German soldier's face in the gloom, arm extended, a rifle in his grip.

The bullet took Bainbridge in the chest, punching him backwards from his feet, where he hit the wall of the pillbox. He dropped to his knees and fumbled to reload his Beholla.

But then a great roaring ocean surged up, and over him, and he remembered no more.

———

On the floor of the pillbox, the wounded German used his rifle to lever himself to his feet, where he swayed for a moment. He looked down at the shot Tommy, face twisting in a grimace of pain. He leant his back against the wall, lifted his rifle, his intention to put another bullet in the body, just to make sure. But then he swayed, and blood-slippery fingers dropped the rifle. He staggered across the pillbox floor and dropped into a seated position beside the machine gun.

His eyes closed. He licked trembling lips. He rested his helmet against the Bergmann with a dull clunk.

Just a short sleep, he thought.

Nobody will miss me. For a few moments.

God, I feel so tired.

Just a short sleep, and I'll wake up back in the Fatherland, away from the mud.

Roman and Elska will stand by my side; I'll take them to

the festival, and I will teach Roman to drink Bockbier. I always said I would teach him to drink Bockbier when he was of age, when he was a man . . .

Sleep came, and with it the darkness of death.

———————

Bainbridge groaned. He could taste metal. There was a spread of damp beneath his coat and he tried to reload his Beholla, but his fingers slipped and fumbled. He felt strength leaving him.

In the distance, the sounds of machine gun fire had lessened, and Bainbridge knew the Allies were close to taking the enemy trench.

But he felt so weak. So tired.

"Don't you dare sleep, you bastard," he growled. "To sleep is to die!"

Gathering his strength and coughing heavily, Bainbridge crawled out of the pillbox and into the rain. It felt good on his face. It felt good to be alive!

The ground was littered with corpses. He crawled over these, teeth gritted and speckled with blood. He'd lost his helmet and could not remember where.

He stopped. Rolled to his back. Listened to the boom of field guns. Enjoyed the cool rain on his fevered flesh.

Where are the stretcher bearers? Those ——ing body

snatchers.

Where the —— are they?

He knew he couldn't reach the trench alone. He coughed again, rolled back to his belly, and heaved his knees beneath him, slopping through mud.

Something moved *within* his chest, sending a fresh wave of agony and nausea slamming through him.

He tried to crawl, but his arms collapsed, and his face pushed into the welcome cool of the earth.

All he could hear was the whistling of crumps as the Fritzies retaliated and set up new lines . . . and screams from the trench behind as blockaded parts brought clashes of hand-to-hand combat to his ears.

So, he was nearby? Near to the German trench?

Where were the others? But . . . of course . . . they would find him, yes, Jones would find him, and the crumps would stop, and everything would be just ——ing fine.

A great grinding, thundering noise came to him; it was close. A flash flickered at the edge of his vision. Heat suddenly scythed across his back and legs, and he fell tumbling into a tombworld of unconsciousness.

———————

Jones crouched in the German trench. The men had

formed a ragged wall of rifles, firing at the retreating German soldiers, rifles crackling like fireworks, watching the Hun sprint across their now-deserted camps, many hitting the ground on their faces as bullets found their mark.

The Tommies moved out, careful, kicking down tents and pushing over barrels and crates with bayonets. Pistols cracked in the distance, leaving echoing reverberations. The machine guns had finally stopped, and smoke curled through the air.

Jones thought briefly about Webb, but he was too busy keeping himself alive.

Webb was on his own.

Jones got to his feet, his rifle at the ready, slippery and cold. Bainbridge had been right: the heavy bombardment of artillery had made the field a treacherous place for an attack.

Something flickered in his mind.

Where was that grumpy old bastard?

To his right, Jones could see the few remaining trees of Polygon Wood rising out of the gloom. Several distant trees provided light as flames soared upwards from their branches.

Flashes from field guns and mortars hidden in the blackened, scorched woods made him half-duck in fear, but the missiles were not too close.

He followed his fellow Tommies across the camp, towards the retreating Hun.

Aiming, his rifle cracked. A German hit the ground, screaming. The sound was lost to Jones.

And all he could think was:

I wish this would all end.

I wish I could go home.

I want to be warm again.

I no longer want to be hunted . . .

DIARY OF ROBERT JONES.
3RD. BATTALION ROYAL WELSH FUSILIERS.
1ST. AUGUST 1917.

I feel dirty. Debased. Impure.

At least I still have my life, as I sit here, alone, shivering by candlelight, wondering where Bainbridge and Webb have got to. I hope they are not dead. Please God, don't let them be dead.

I will tour the hospitals soon. Maybe I'll find them there. I hope so. I pray.

I was going to write down my experiences during the assault, but what's the point now? It's all been written before, so many glorified accounts, soldiers, warriors, heroes. No matter how grim a picture I paint, there will always be those who have bright excited eyes, who think War is romantic, exciting, a beast to be tamed. I learnt about the pleasures of life the hard way; life in a sanatorium when you are a boy is not an enjoyable experience. Four years. Four years of my life in that stinking rat hole . . . but rather a life in a sanatorium than here in the trenches. Strangely, the two experiences are similar. The stench. The cold. Only here the enemy are the Hun, men like you and me . . . whereas inside the sanatorium, the enemy was within us, around us in the guise of warders and inmates and the scum who used to beat me through pillows held against my back so as to leave no bruising . . .

I will not write of the battle. Once, six months ago, I was sick to death of war. That sickness has passed, and now I feel only emptiness. I cannot have dreams. How can I have dreams for the future, when I could die at any moment? How can I dream of going back to Sarah, apologising, making it right again, marriage, having children—children! Future bullet fodder, to be used by this great machine of War.

I apologise. My thoughts are dark.

I will go and look for George. I will look for Bainbridge as well—I only hope they have lived through this madness. But how will I explain to Marie if her brother has died?

How?

YPRES SALIENT (3RD. BATTLE OF).

"NO MAN'S LAND."

2ND. AUGUST 1917 (EARLY MORNING).

IT WAS THE COLD of ice, the cold of the grave, the cold of the tombworld. The iciness had passed, beyond pain and mere discomfort. This was heart-deep and filled Webb's mind with a numbing ferocity; it blanketed the fear and the pain, and when he groaned, his lower lip cracked open with blood trickling down his chin.

Water. He needed water.

He tried to open his eyes, but they were nailed shut. He coughed, a pitiful wheezing, and moved a hand, ever so slowly, and cried out as it brushed something sharp and a fresh wave of pain flowed into his mind, his core, and he screamed silently, mouth open, no sounds emerging as the fire fought the ice across his eyes and through his skull and down the back of his neck and down his spine . . .

When he awoke, he was warmer. Damp. He moved his hand again—the pain biting him like a dog—and fumbled for his canteen, but it was gone. He moved his hand to his face, opened his eyes, opened his eyes into . . .

Darkness.

"I'm blind."

His voice was soft, calm, touched with a deep sadness and a fear rooted in his soul. His fingers gently brushed against the weeping flesh of his cheek. And he realised why the cold had left him ... it was blood, his blood, soaking him.

He reached behind himself, could feel the jutting splinters of sharp metal, slippery under fingers, poking from his back and rib cage; obscene metal erections digging, piercing into flesh ... he managed to get a grip on one piece, but it bit him, and he did not have the strength to pull it free.

"You ——er."

The effort left him panting, licking cracked and bleeding lips. He eased himself onto his belly and lay there, burnt cheek in the cool mud, soothing him, bathing him with its purity.

"Mother?"

She stood beside him, he knew. She was talking to him, her words sweet and beautiful, despite her coughing and pain-filled voice. She was soothing him with her love. She was praying for him.

"Don't pray for me, Mother."

She prayed anyway. And then reached out, her fingers curling between Webb's fingers, her hand warm and comforting, somehow holy. Webb started to cry, but she soothed his tears, and the pure mud took them into the ground, to be part of the earth, part of the world.

She was talking to him, but her words seemed strange, alien, and he could not understand her. Her voice crackled and hissed, like the whispering leaves of the trees, the creak of branches, the scuff of bark on bark.

He could feel her, feel the cleansed flesh of her body, and she was no longer dying, no longer had the cancer, and she would live, yes! she would live and would take him back home to England and there she would nurse him back to health as she had done so many times when he was a little boy and she would no longer be weak no longer riddled with horror and the promise of death no she would be fit and healthy and the beautiful mother he knew from his youth before diseases of flesh caught her in their terrible snare . . .

"Mother, hold me," he whimpered.

And she held him, her arms encircling his body, pressing lightly against the shrapnel in his flesh and making him scream. He screamed loud and long. And wept. And yet, at the same time, he wanted to laugh, so great was his joy, so great was his hope, and the two feelings fought for precedence until they mingled in an almost orgasmic feeling of warmth and comfort which filled his body and mind and soul right down to the roots of the world . . .

The rain woke him, pounding him.

Webb's mother had gone.

He tried to blink, but the movement brought only pain.

Shit. She had gone. Now he felt only emptiness.

Water soaked Webb's hair and trickled down his cheeks, cooling his flesh, and he could feel the coldness of the metal in his body, an alien intrusion.

Fight, he told himself.

Do it for your mother . . .

And he knew what he had to do: he had to get back to the trench. That was where she waited. Her spirit. Her reborn flesh. She would be there for him. She would help him. She would take him home and nurse him and everything would be all right again.

Rain hammered him. Fell heavy.

Webb rolled to his back, driving shrapnel deeper, and a scream burst from cracked and bloody lips, loud, deafening, echoing out over No Man's Land, a wail, a song, a song for No Man's Land which pierced the silence and darkness and horror and mud and the very veil of death which hung over this place.

He gritted his teeth, and with an intense show of obstinacy, and pride, and anger, he heaved himself to his hands and knees, ignoring the pain and the fire as he clenched his fists deep into the churned mud and blood, nausea filling him with bile.

Webb breathed deep. He was breathing. He was alive.

He started to crawl through the mud, struggling against the pain within and the elements without; suddenly, his hand came up against something hard and cold and rough. He stopped. He lifted his hand to the rough texture; caressed it.

Concrete.

He laughed. It was a pillbox.

But which way to the Allied trench?

His laugh faded quick.

What would happen if he travelled the wrong way and in blindness found himself over the Huns' wires? He would never reach his mother, never find peace, never be warm, never return home.

Think. Think!

The pillbox—the *German* pillbox—that was the answer. It would have slots on the side facing the Allies, and a doorway to the rear. Slowly, Webb worked his hands up the concrete face, grunting as the metal in his flesh grated against two ribs and fired him with fresh waves of washing, undulating pain. But he could not feel anything under his fingertips . . .

Too low. Too low.

He would have to stand up. He would have to do

the one thing which was beyond him . . . and in grim determination, he dug his cracked and broken nails into the chipped concrete and started to heave, his panting now coming in shallow bursts, his eyes blinking despite the pain this caused, salt sweat stinging the wounds on his back, tears coursing down his torn cheeks as biceps screamed protest and his back screamed white agony and his body wailed the song which echoed around his skull, caged, locked inside, and his fingers scrabbled against the firing aperture just as his legs buckled and he fell away onto his face, and welcomed the blackness as an end to pain.

———————

Webb slept for a million years. In his dreams, he flowed down to the roots of the world, entwined with the very bedrock of the planet.

He awoke.

The rain continued to drum against his twisted helmet. He opened his mouth and welcomed the water into his parched throat, soothing his lips and tongue and cheeks and eyes—ah, the bliss of cool rain on damaged eyelids!

The pain had receded. It had become a weary demon within him. He managed to climb to his knees and began to crawl again, this time sure of his direction, sure of his destination; this fired him with vigour, hope, and the last remnants of belief.

He encountered bodies as he crawled. Both ally and enemy, he could tell by groping at their helmets, their uniforms, and he managed to find himself a knife which he tucked into his damaged belt with shaking fingers.

He crawled over the bodies, finding it easier to go over than around, using their stiffened limbs as handholds to drag himself forward.

And as he crawled, he heard the voice. It was weeping softly, then growling in anger, then crying, "Father, you bastard, I curse you!" in words filled with phlegm and spitting and loathing . . .

Webb crawled on. The voice shifted closer. "Hey!" shouted Webb, although his own voice was shaky, a barely audible croak.

The cursing subsided. The owner of the voice became silent.

Webb crawled in the direction of the voice, over more broken bodies, through the dragging mud. The drumming of rain on his helmet began to drive him mad, so with one hand he tugged it off and flung it away, where it splashed into invisible gloom.

"Is that you, Webb?" Webb didn't recognise the voice, for the words were spoken slow, through clenched teeth.

"Yes," he managed, eventually, crawling towards the figure, and bumping into him, then slumping to the mud by the man's side. "My name's Webb."

They lay there for about a minute, neither speaking. "Are you wounded?" managed Webb. The man laughed, a sound that bubbled in his lungs.

"Aye. I am that."

Webb ran a hand across his forehead, then asked, "Is it still night?" But even as he asked the words, a soft light started to filter into his vision. He had been damaged, but his eyesight was beginning to return.

"No. Early morning. It will be dawn soon. And the gunners will see us."

More silence. The man started to groan softly. "This is awful, Webb. I can't stand this pain. It's eating me. It's ——ing eating me . . ."

"Who are you? Do I know you?"

Webb frowned, trying to ignore his own pain, trying to ignore the feeling of utter despair in this wounded soldier's voice. And then the man spoke again, and his words tore through Webb's lack of clarity.

"Bainbridge," said the man, his voice still strange, alien. "And I'm proper dying, lad. Got a serious belly-ache!" Even as he spoke he coughed, and laughed, and tiny droplets spattered Webb's face.

Webb flinched. Then, gently, he reached out and took

Bainbridge's hand. He felt for a pulse in the wrist. It was weak. Fluttering. "The body snatchers will find us," whispered Webb.

But Bainbridge had passed into unconsciousness, and Webb sat for a while, his own pain distant, remembering Bainbridge's words of anger back in the trench, words of hatred spat from angered lips, the jibes, the put-downs, the pain . . . pain of the mind, pain of the soul.

"I hate you," said Webb in the rain, smiling, looking down at Bainbridge with damaged eyes. He could picture the man's face in his mind, with a snarl, or a grimace of anger . . . and he could not find a memory of Bainbridge with a smile.

"Are you there?" Bainbridge's hand came up suddenly, gripped Webb's arm, his grip tight, his fingers clammy and cold. "Are you there, Father? I hate you, I hate your ——ing whining, your pitiful moans. Can't you leave me alone now? I'm dying, damn you . . . Leave me to die in peace."

"Bainbridge?" Webb's voice was soft.

"Shut up; I'll never forgive you, you bastard . . ." And then he started to cry, sobs shaking his huge frame, and moving closer, Webb stroked Bainbridge's hair and cradled the giant sergeant's head in his lap.

"Be calm," he said.

"I didn't mean it." More tears. "You make me angry. I

didn't mean it . . . I love you, really, love you to death. I'd do anything for you. Please don't shout."

Webb sat for many minutes, silent, mouth a grim line as Bainbridge rambled aimlessly, talking to soldiers long dead, talking to a father long gone, making peace with himself; making peace with his soul.

Webb felt great sadness descend on his shoulders. He no longer had hate within him. Once, he wished Bainbridge dead. But now he saw that for what it was. Bainbridge was simply a man who was lost and alone, a man filled with anger and pride, now reduced to whimpering like a babe in Webb's arms.

Suddenly, Bainbridge went quiet.

Webb shook him.

"Don't die on me, Bainbridge, don't you ——ing die on me! Come on, talk to me! I'm here to listen! They'll find us soon, I promise, find us and carry us back to the trench."

"George?"

The word was said with such calm that Webb jumped.

"Yes, Sergeant?"

"I'm sorry . . . about what I called you. You aren't a . . . coward, lad. I'm sorry."

"Forget it."

"I . . . I cannot forget. It's burning me, boy, can't you see? I had too much anger. You understand?"

"I understand."

"I just wanted to hurt everyone. It's this place. It changed me. I . . . I've done so many foolish things. I've hurt so many people. Can you see that?"

"Yes," whispered Webb, nodding, waiting for Bainbridge to continue. But Bainbridge lay back, wincing in pain, his breathing fast and shallow.

Webb didn't know what to do. But slowly, as the dawn broke, so his vision returned to some semblance of clarity. He could see blasted trees. Torn stone walls. A smashed house, only two walls still standing.

Bainbridge's breathing was like an erratic rhythm.

"I need to get help," muttered Webb, and gently he laid the wounded sergeant in the mud. He forced himself to his knees and looked around, tried to work out the direction of the Allied trench. And as he looked up, he saw three large figures, shrouded in black, their glittering eyes watching, their muzzles curled in amusement.

"We found you," said one.

"Just look at them squirm," said another.

"More meat for our machine."

Webb stared, unsure of what he was looking at. They wore German uniforms, helmets merging with flesh, and yet their faces were very far from human. They carried Hun rifles, and Webb's observation finished by fixating on the dark, gleaming bayonets.

They moved forward then, lifting their rifles, their muzzles drooling, their eyes hard and alien. Webb's hands came up as if to ward off attack, but they stepped past him, and all three surrounded Bainbridge.

Bainbridge opened his eyes. He grinned a grin of violence.

"What are you ugly mothers staring at?" he snarled.

One walrider thrust forward, and its bayonet skewered Bainbridge's shoulder. He screamed, kicking his legs, but was pinned there by the bayonet. There was a *crack* as his clavicle snapped.

"No!" screamed Webb, launching to his feet, launching *at* the creatures, but a walrider turned and backhanded him savagely, claws scoring deep lines across Webb's cheek, nearly tearing it free in a big flap of skin and pissing blood. Webb was sent spinning up, over, slammed into the mud.

They turned their attention back to Bainbridge. The large Tommy was laughing from a mask of blood.

"Is that all you've got?" he gurgled. "Even my sister could take you down, you feeble little maggots."

The other two walriders plunged in bayonets, one piercing Bainbridge's chest, one piercing his throat. They stood there, their massive figures immobile, their rifles extensions of their evil, the three slivers of steel slicing through flesh and muscle and tendon and bone.

Bainbridge convulsed. One leg kicked. And he went terribly still, there in the mud.

————————

Maybe it was a dream. A nightmare. Possibly a vision from heaven, or hell. All Webb understood was that he *was* there, floating in the cool breeze, gazing down from a great height, seeking his comrades in the murk far below.

He felt like a bird. A bird spirit that had emerged from the darkness after a hundred years of solitude. He desperately needed company; he searched for his friends but found only death.

He floated in the breeze. It ruffled his hair, filled his senses with its perfume. The pain had gone. He reached behind himself but could find no intrusion of metal.

He was healed.

And he could see with perfect clarity!

He drank in the land like wine, revelled in the vision swimming before him. It was ecstasy made real, a solid thing he could see and touch and feel. And yet he gazed down on nothing alive. Everything was slaughter. Everything was destruction.

The dawn crept near, like a frightened child.

Singular strands of solid light oozed across a distant infinity. Below, solid black stalks reared towards the sky, and towards God, like accusatory fingers. The dead trees pointed, in their embrace of oblivion, ugly, charred, and hopeless.

A desecration.

Debris littered the ground between the dead tree trunks and the corpses. Abandoned crates. Boots. Old duckboards and rusting barbed wire. The corpses themselves were twisted, horrible, unholy, mouths open, gaping silent curses at God and Hell and Man. They were mud-streaked, and bloodied, and broken, and bent like tossed marionettes. Their blasted, excised veins were strings and they danced a jig in honour of a race cursed by its own self-harming hand.

He watched. Smoke flowed across the battlefield. Grey smoke, thin, empty of substance, like gruel. Looking left and right, he could see no life. It was as if he embraced another realm, as if he had been carried by the angels to a plane of existence one step above life . . . and the smoke flowed over the bodies, Germans and French, British and Americans, Australians and Belgians . . . The smoke curled lazily across the corpses, and as he watched, he could see it grow and dance and then solidify with each passing spiral. As if each man, lying twisted in horror, was adding an essence to the whole, becoming a glorious unity, a celebration of life rather than a condemnation of death.

He flew then, faster than light, speeding down, seeking friends and enemies, searching faces amongst the nameless, frozen ranks of countless bodies. But their souls had gone, passed away to some higher place, leaving flesh shells like hollow trees, broken bark, smashed wooden totems of innocence and futility laid out on the ground between the chipped pillboxes, between churned trenches, between the wire and the shell holes and the shit.

He was dragged free and lifted above the smoke. The land was desolate below him, littered with husks of wood, corpses carved from the earth and returning to the earth. He could hear their song, hear their heartsong, as they joined the eternal spirit and the wind sighed in the heavens and the souls sped with laughter, singing, singing their song for No Man's Land.

Pain speared him. Reality came crashing back.

He coughed blood, which dribbled down his chin.

He could hear voices—muffled, as through a dark green ocean.

He tried to move but could not.

Felt himself sinking, spiralling down into the graveworld.

YPRES SALIENT (3RD. BATTLE OF).

"TRUTH."

2ND. AUGUST 1917 (EARLY MORNING).

A PIT IN THE EARTH. Webb crawled in. Curled up. Wished for death. He could still hear Bainbridge's death cries. Still see the walriders, their bayonets piercing the large Tommy's flesh.

"You bastards," he muttered. "You bastards."

And then a voice. A voice he thought impossible. A voice from dark dreams . . .

Webb was lying foetal, the shrapnel in his side and back disguised by black mud. He screamed, and Jones placed a hand on his friend's head, dropped his rifle, and took the man's hand, squeezing it in reassurance.

"George? It's me, Robert. I'm here to take you back. You're going home to Wales, lad. Your time in the war is over."

"It's too late, too late," whispered Webb.

"No, man, you'll be okay," Jones lied, swallowing hard and holding back tears.

"Was she beautiful, Robert? Beautiful?"

"Who, George?"

"My mother. When you saw her at the end. Did she glow, like all the angels?"

"Yes. She glowed, my friend."

Webb screamed again, then lay moaning, unmoving. Jones gave a quick glance across No Man's Land. They were sitting targets out there in the gloom. Sitting ——ing ducks.

"I can't move, Robert. I can't move!"

"It's okay; it's just shock." Jones hated himself for the lie, for he had seen the shrapnel in Webb's back, sharp iron slicing close to Webb's spine. "You'll recover soon, lad. We'll have a drink in the pub and laugh about old times."

"Where's Bainbridge? Did you see Bainbridge?"

"Here, let me help you."

With all his strength, Jones hoisted Webb up, grabbed his rifle, and slid and crawled up the slope of the shell hole. He stood there, with flares lighting the sky, and the flash of crumps sparking in the distance. Bullets clattered. Tanks droned.

A cool wind blew across No Man's Land. It carried the gentle symphony of war.

And then Jones saw them. Three huge figures. The beasts which hunted him.

His eyes went hard, and his jaw went tight.

"I'm just going to put you down here for a minute,

Webb," he said, lowering his wounded friend to the mud.

"Oh, my God," breathed Webb. "It's them!" Jones glanced at him. "They murdered Bainbridge. Stabbed him to death with their bayonets . . ."

Jones narrowed his eyes. "Well, it's time somebody taught them a lesson," he growled, and his rifle came up, and he started to fire, operating the bolt, firing again. Bullets whined across No Man's Land, impacting with the huge figures who lowered their heads, muzzles drooling, and charged, their own rifles spitting fire and bullets . . .

They were a terrible sight. Webb watched, whimpering, from the ground.

The creatures powered forward, unstoppable, demons of mud and flesh and stolen Hun form.

Jones leapt forward, a final bullet crashing into the face of a walrider, punching it back from its feet, where its legs started to kick. A huge fist full of claws and skin like bark crashed into Jones's head, but he spun with the blow, his rifle sweeping out and back, the bayonet slicing across a leg, cutting fabric, slicing skin and bone. The walrider screamed. Jones came up fast, leaping at a beast, his fist hitting its muzzle, snapping a yellow fang, slicing his knuckle to the bone. But the third walrider leapt on his back, bearing him down. He slammed his head back, once, twice, three times, snapping fangs like twigs, but its weight was too great. Something hit Jones in the back of the head, and stars spun through his skull, and he groaned, tasting grit, tasting mud, tasting blood.

"——."

Big, powerful hands, claws, turned him over. He was blind for a moment. A walrider sat astride him, its weight crushing. It was grinning, leering down at him.

"Your time has come, Robert Jones," it said, and pulled out a pistol. The black barrel stared at Jones like a dark final eye.

He started to struggle, thrashing, his fists slamming blows against the beast astride him. The others chuckled, their drool falling to the mud.

"We'll count to three," said a beast.

"And shoot you in the face," said another, its face leering out of the smoke-filled gloom.

"One."

"Two."

"Three!"

A bayonet point erupted from the throat of the walrider astride Jones, then twisted viciously. It sawed for a moment, revealing a raw, bobbing Adam's apple, then cut sideways in a vicious slice and jerk of power. The head toppled sideways from the body, revealing the blood-drenched figure of Bainbridge, rifle in both hands, swaying, blood pumping from the wounds in his throat, chest and shoulder.

"Is that all you've ——ing got?" he bubbled, blood pouring down his chin, and then fell sideways in the mud.

Jones rolled to his knees, grabbed Bainbridge's rifle, pulled free his knife, and attacked. A bullet took the first beast through the mouth on an upwards trajectory and exploded the top of its head in a shower of skull shards and pulped brain. It stared at Jones for a few moments, jaws working spasmodically, then its eyes seemed to fill with humour as it looked *past* Jones to the final beast . . . and then it collapsed.

Jones whirled about, saw the rifle lift, heard the discharge. A bullet whined past his ear. As if in slow motion, he watched the creature operate the bolt, its eyes locked on him. *You're mine now,* said those eyes. *Worm food.*

Webb reared behind it and with a scream plunged his bayonet in the walrider's back. It grunted, blood spraying from its mouth, and tried to turn. Then claws slashed out, a backward punch, connecting with Webb's face, breaking his cheekbone, sending him flailing to the ground . . .

Jones ran and leapt, his knife punching into the walrider's throat. But still it fought, and a fist crashed against his head like a hammer blow. He hit the mud, and looked up as the wounded walrider reared above him, claws flexing, murder in its glittering eyes.

And then something . . . miraculous happened.

Jones felt the power of the earth surge through him. It felt like tree roots, winding around his feet, then up, entwining his legs, entering him through his very flesh, winding tightly around his bones and tendons and *strengthening him* and he felt the power of the Skogsgrå *inside his very flesh and body and soul.*

Jones stood, and the walrider charged. It punched, claws hissing, and he blocked, then twisted his arm, breaking the walrider's. It screamed, and Jones punched out, his fist entering the beast's face, and punching *through* to exit in a shower of blood. In his fist, he held its brain.

Jones let go.

And then he blinked.

The walrider fell to the earth, its muzzle gone, its face a platter of bloody pulp.

Jones breathed. Felt the Skogsgrå leave him . . .

And it was over.

———

Voices. Alien, grinding, guttural, as if the very trees had decided to talk.

"Be careful . . . slowly, now!"

"Shit. Look at that . . . I'm surprised he's still ——ing breathing!"

"Just get him on the stretcher and keep your thoughts to yourself. And for God's sake, be careful of the shrapnel. Slowly, now . . . careful does it . . ."

"What about the other one?"

"Put him on a stretcher."

"But he's dead."

"Put him on a ——ing stretcher!"

"He's ——ing dead!"

"Do you want to join him? Well, do as I say, and stop your ——ing whining. Both of these men are going back to the trenches with me, and I'll kill any bastard who stands in my way."

——————

The pain came, filled Webb up as if he were a jug, and left him screaming on the canvas stretcher, writhing like a scorched worm. The stretcher-bearers backed away as if stung, but not Jones. Jones was there, kneeling in the mud, his rifle in one hand, eyes scanning the field then looking down into the face of George Webb, with his blood-filled eyes and savagely torn face.

"How . . . how is Bainbridge?"

"He's dead," said Jones. His cheeks were wet.

"Yes. I forgot. He died like a hero. Brave to the end! A warrior!"

"Both of you," smiled Jones. "Both heroes."

The stretcher bearers exchanged glances.

There was silence, then Webb coughed, blood frothing at his chin.

"I can feel the metal in my body. It hurts so much . . . I can see her! She's calling to me . . . she's calling for me to join her!"

"Go to her," whispered Jones.

"She looks so beautiful. Can you see her?"

"I can see her," said Jones.

"Isn't she beautiful?"

"Yes. She's beautiful."

"Don't leave me here, Rob. Don't leave me in all this mud. Don't leave me in this . . . in this wasteland."

"I won't. One day, Webb, we'll go back to glorious Wales! You remember the mountains, don't you? The sunlight glinting from rock and slate? The towering, watchful eyes? You remember the forests, and the valleys, don't you Webb? Wales, the most beautiful country in the world."

Webb closed his eyes and coughed, and Jones wiped the blood from his friend's chin with his handkerchief. Tears ran down his own face, and Webb started to heave as if to vomit, but he settled back, fingers twitching, working feverishly.

Jones looked up, looked around at the stretcher-bearers, who stared with faces of grave desolation. Jones used his Lee-Enfield to lever himself to his feet, then gazed down at Webb struggling at the border of life and death.

So much pain, he thought. *So much pain.*

He had to put an end to it.

Webb started to moan, blood bubbling in his lungs, and Jones lifted his rifle and the shot split the silence in two, split the world in half on its axis.

Jones glanced at the body snatchers, eyes challenging, waiting for words . . . but they did not come.

A soft glow seemed to surround Webb, and Jones stood, rifle in trembling blood-stained hands, his mouth dropping open. Suddenly, a tiny shoot appeared in the mud and was quickly joined by a hundred others. Swiftly they grew, winding, wavering stalks, and then petals opened into the beautiful bright bloom of a red poppy; into hundreds of red poppies.

Jones watched, turning, and this sudden surge of flowers spread across the mud like a swift-growing carpet of red, until they surrounded Bainbridge and filled the air with a glorious scent.

In the distance, the guns stopped.

A deathly silence fell like ash.

Jones moved to Bainbridge and knelt by his dead friend. He placed his hand on the big Tommy's breast and said a silent prayer, inhaling the poppies, his face showing rapture and awe.

"What about . . . these?" said a stretcher bearer, eventually, his words trembling, as he gestured to the dead walriders. Jones met their stares and gave a nasty grin.

"Do you think anybody would believe you?"

One man shook his head.

"And the poppies? Would they believe what you'd tell them?"

"No."

"My advice? Keep your mouth shut. Now back to the trenches," he said, voice hoarse with grief.

In silence, they gathered the bodies of Jones's friends and moved across No Man's Land, careful, watchful, with Jones taking the rear, unable to look at the corpses they carried.

He could feel a dull ache in his heart, which nagged him and made him feel cold and alone, and he shivered, and he was sweating at the same time and the pain inside him radiated outwards, ate at him like gnashing metal teeth; like roaring machine gun bullets; ate his body, and ate his soul.

But at least you killed them, he thought.

At least you killed the Hunters.

DIARY OF ROBERT JONES.
3RD. BATTALION ROYAL WELSH FUSILIERS.
6TH. AUGUST 1917.

I have lost all hope. I am alone. I am alone in this darkest of Hell. I sit here and know not what to write; my pen scratches slow on the page, I am confused, I am wracked with grief. My friends are gone, dead, my best friends lying under sacking waiting to be buried in a mass grave. I must write to Marie soon, tell her about George, tell her how he died a heroic death—lie about how he fell in glorious battle, eyes shining with pride and honour, and how he died without pain. He died with very much pain, I saw the wounds, the blind eyes, the shrapnel lodged in his back. But I must lie. I must lie to protect the innocent, so as to bring just a little comfort out of the trenches. The trenches—furrows in the devil's spine, in which we crouch, awaiting his loving touch.

I miss Sarah. Miss her with all my heart and soul.

Bainbridge. What did I really know about him? I know little of his childhood. Nothing of his dreams, his desires, his longings. So I find myself with the difficult task of penning thoughts which flow disjointedly in my head, thoughts of war and guns and our time together in France. Perhaps not, though. Perhaps I will just leave their shadows as a memory. And when I die, then we will all be silent heroes together, beyond the grave.

I am haunted. Haunted by the bullet that killed Webb. I have started to tell myself maybe he would have lived, survived, if we'd just brought him back to the trench. By shooting him—no matter my reasons for ending his pain—by shooting him I simply extinguished a life that could have flared bright and pure.

God is to blame. God, and Man.

It's all gone wrong. An insane game. The biggest that's played, right? And what was it for? What was it all ——ing for? Nothing. Nothing at all.

YPRES SALIENT (3RD. BATTLE OF).
"THE TRENCHES."
11TH. AUGUST 1917.

JONES STOOD ALONE on a hilltop, a cold wind caressing him, howling softly, like a funeral song. He felt strange, alive for the first time in years. Nothing else mattered. He stood there, looking down on civilisation below, on the lights of a culture which no longer belonged, a world which had cast him into the breach and pumped him like a shell into the dark razors of war.

Lights glittered, shimmering. Distant sounds flowed on the breeze. Shouts. Laughter. *Life.*

He turned, and looked down the opposite side of the hill, two different sides of the same coin: below, the silence was shattered by mortar shells and gunfire. Flares lit up the sky. Men screamed in the mud as they were sliced down by a scything blade of hot bullets.

The smile faded from Jones's face. He felt utterly alone, in body, mind, and soul.

"Come and warm yourself by my fire."

Jones turned and glanced at the nearby trees, a vibrant gathering of silver birch and sycamore. A small clearing stood close by, and a fire burned, the flames more colourful than anything Jones had ever seen.

A figure sat by the fire, features cast in shadow, watching.

Jones walked across the hilltop, treading through a field of poppies which danced, bright red, in the breeze.

He ducked under the low canopy and moved towards the fire, where the figure gestured to a fire-warmed rock. Jones sat, stone hard beneath his flesh, real and uncompromising.

"Welcome."

"This is a dream," said Jones, eyes locking to the eyes of Bainbridge. "You are a dream, my friend."

Bainbridge smiled. "We are all dreams, Jones. The whole world is a dream. I am in your thoughts, which is all that matters. It is proof that you have not forgotten me. Proof you have not gone insane."

"How could I forget you? You were my friend!"

Bainbridge nodded.

"This is insane," said Jones, frowning, "you are in my fevered imagination, *dead,* so how the —— can I be holding this conversation?"

"The soul is a strange creature, lad. It has many facets, like a diamond. Some are smooth, some rough. Some have many floors, many different layers. And some of those layers are invisible to the naked eye. Think about it,

Robert. Think about it."

"What do you mean?"

Fear.

Bainbridge smiled, harsh face becoming kind. "Why did you shoot Webb, lad? Answer me that."

————

Jones awoke suddenly, shivering, his blankets on the floor. Leaning from his bunk, he snatched at the covers, pulled the rough, itchy fabric over his body, huddling beneath their poor protection willing warmth back into his limbs.

"Damn."

He reached out, found the flask Bainbridge used to hide under his bunk, and twisted off the cap. There was only a single mouthful of whisky inside, but it was enough. Jones drank it down and lay back, shaking, and wondering how much his shivers were attributed to cold.

"You're dead, Bainbridge," he said. "You're ——ing dead."

The wooden walls answered him with silence. He pictured Webb, again, writhing in the mud, blood bubbling at his lips.

"Why? I did it for mercy. I did it because he'd suffered enough. He might have lived another hour, maybe a day.

But Webb would have died, Bainbridge. And I know you understand that, wherever you are."

Gradually, Jones fell asleep, only this time he was calm, now his breathing was regular, and No Man's Land could not haunt him, death could not haunt him, and he slept.

In his dreams, he dreamt about endless fields of poppies.

———————

The next day, whistles sang, a haunting song of desolation.

And Jones went over the bags.

Went over the bags alone.

THE SANATORIUM.
"A CANOPY OF SILVER DREAMS."
JANUARY 1904.

THE LANTERNS CAST a gentle, ethereal glow around the stark white room. The boy sat, nervous, huddled in the space of a large hardwood chair, eyes frightened as they darted about the room.

A figure entered. A man. A doctor.

He stood motionless in the doorframe for perhaps a minute, then, lighting a cigarette, he locked the door and pocketed the key in his expensive grey suit. Strolling to the desk, he sat down, leaned back, put his heels up on the wooden desk, and orientated on the boy huddled in the chair, eyes red-rimmed from crying.

"Tell me about it."

The boy did not answer.

"You mentioned names. Hunter's Hill. Sharpwood. Clearwood. What are the names *for*? Where did they come from?" The man frowned when no response was forthcoming, and slamming his fist on the table-top, making a lantern rattle, he hissed, "Come on, now, boy..." He paused, thinking, and with forcible effort, calmed his tone. "You want to go home, don't you?"

The boy looked up. Ah, that had an effect!

"It was in the woods. It *was* the woods," said the boy, words a murmur, eyes staring at the floor.

"Explain."

The man drew on his cigarette, blew blue smoke into the air, allowed the smoke to curl outwards. The boy searched inside his own head for the words to tell the man, words to explain this demon of his fears made real. The struggle. The hunting. The huge carvings, speaking to him with long-dead mouths . . .

You will come to us, they said.

One day, you will fight with us.

One day, you will save us.

"I can't," he whispered, finally.

"Try. You did well last week."

"I can't. Not now."

Lantern light danced against the walls, demonic pagan figures whirling and laughing, illuminated in red.

The man finished his cigarette and moved to the boy, touching his cheek where it was flushed red from crying.

"I want my mother," whimpered the child.

"Well, we all want things in life," said the doctor, face hard, and, closing his eyes, lifted his face to the ceiling. "But in this world, boy, you are expected to cooperate to get what you want. Understand? Start talking, and maybe your life will improve in this place. Perhaps."

There came a knock at the door.

"Yes?" he snapped, exasperated.

"There is someone to see you, Doctor."

The man smiled, a smile without humour—a smile which belonged on a devil's face, a devil's sick of sin. He patted the boy's shoulder and removed the key from his pocket. "I'll be back later," he said, and his smile was devoid of friendship or warmth. He left the room, locking the door behind him.

———————

The boy lay on his bunk in the depths of the sanatorium ward. It was dark, and cold, and smelled of strong disinfectant and puke. He could hear strange sounds: pipes rattling; the stealthy footfalls of the night sister, padding; people breathing; children sleeping; the occasional cough; the occasional clatter; the occasional whimper of fear.

He lay with eyes closed, face lifted to the ceiling. The pillows were damp from his tears. The blankets were coarse and itchy. His bladder was full, but he did not dare get out to use the bedpan. The nurse would be angry. And she was a demon when she was angry. More alien than alien.

A cool breeze soothed over him, like silk.

He dreamed of running through the trees, through the rain, through Clearwood, over the terrible obstacles of Sharpwood, and towards Hunter's Hill. There, he would be free again. There, he would be whole again, despite the creatures which hunted him. He understood them now. They were a barrier. A protection, grown by the ancient woodland . . . to keep out . . . intruders.

And he was not an intruder.

He understood that now.

He was . . . a *part* of the woods. A part of the story. A part of the fabric.

"Wake."

"Mm?"

"Awake," came the breath, colder than the grave.

The boy's eyes flickered open. He had been asleep after all. He jumped, for at the foot of his bed, perched on the brass rail with clenched claws, was the Skogsgrå. She was big, bigger than any man he had ever seen. Her eyes were large grey discs, staring at him. Her limbs were sinewy, like cords of torn, twisted timber. Her flesh was silver bark. Her long hair was a flowing carpet of moss. Her eyes were knots, her nose holes in the gently grained wood of her face. Her fingers were like branches, her toes thorn claws which gripped the brass bedrail, crushing it.

"Don't hurt me!"

"I am not here to hurt you."

"Don't kill me!"

"If I wanted you dead, you'd be dead already."

Her voice was like the whispering of leaves on an autumn evening. Her vowels were the brush of branches. Her consonants were the creak of boughs in a rough winter wind.

The boy looked nervously about the ward. Everything was still. Silent. Trapped in a pocket of time.

"What do you want?" he squeaked, voice tiny, blankets clutched under his chin like armour.

"We want *you*," breathed the Skogsgrå.

"Why? To kill me?"

"Not at all." The face twisted into something horrific, something he could only imagine from tales of horror, stories of Hell, demons from a dark and deviant imagination. Bad stuff. *Evil* stuff. And then the boy realised . . . she was *smiling*. The Skogsgrå was smiling.

"What, then?"

"Let me tell you a story. It's about a little boy who feels a calling. He feels it in his flesh, in his bones, in his very soul. And he faces great odds to answer that calling, because it is a part of him, something deeper than life or death, deeper than parents or religion. And he understands, intrinsically, that in life, there are things one must do. Things that are right. Battles one must fight. Elements of the very fabric of the world which are not . . . good, and must be put right, no matter what the cost."

"I don't understand."

"Robert Jones. A great war is coming. Not in one world, but in two. They cross one another, run in parallel, and yet intertwine—like strands of cotton, woven together to form a braid. You will be caught up in this war—not in one world but both. And when things get bad, so bad you think it will never end, we *will* come for you, and we will do our best to help. To put an end to this atrocity. To stop this scourge against life."

The boy had tears on his cheeks. He shook his head. "Why me? What could I possibly do?"

"You will be a hero," growled the Skogsgrå, "but more importantly, you will strive to do what is right. For your people . . . and for mine."

"You are part of the woods? The ancient trees?"

The Skogsgrå nodded, with a creak of timber.

"When will you come for me?"

The Skogsgrå smiled.

"Why," she said, jumping backwards from the crushed brass bedrail, and landing with a clatter of thorns on the sterile, polished sanatorium tiles. "On the day that you die, of course."

ACKNOWLEDGMENTS

Thanks to my little boys, Joe and Olly, for making me laugh so much! Thanks to Sonia, for all the good times, to Roy, for his filmmaking enthusiasm, and to my test-readers and proofreaders—I-owe-you-all-many-beers!! Thanks to John Jarrold, for his advice and pub lunches, and to Lee Harris at Tor for his unending support.

About the Author

Photograph by Joseph Remic

ANDY REMIC started his author career writing high-octane science fiction novels but soon graduated to epic fantasy. His writing is relentless, passionate, visceral. It's the literary equivalent of an extreme sport and should come with a government health warning. Described by many as the natural successor to David Gemmell, Remic enjoys pummeling his readers with scene after scene of action and mayhem. He also enjoys pummeling his characters.

You'll never be bored with a Remic novel!

www.andyremic.com

TOR·COM

Science fiction. Fantasy. The universe.

And related subjects.

*

More than just a publisher's website, *Tor.com*

is a venue for **original fiction, comics,** and

discussion of the entire field of SF and fantasy,

in all media and from all sources. Visit our site

today — and join the conversation yourself.